A Journey into Time

and
Other
Stories

GRACE STORMS TOWER

Illustrated by Eric von Schmidt

United Church Press Boston • Philadelphia

The scripture quotations in this book are from the *Revised Standard Version of the Bible,* copyrighted 1946 and 1952, and from the *Revised Standard Version of the Apocrypha,* copyrighted 1957 by the Division of Christian Education of the National Council of Churches. Used by permission.

This book is part of the United Church Curriculum, prepared and published by the Division of Christian Education and the Division of Publication of the United Church Board for Homeland Ministries.

Table of Contents

ABOUT THIS BOOK

If a Palestinian boy or girl of two thousand years ago were to come to life in your town today, he would find it a very strange and unfamiliar place. Almost everything would be new to him—television, automobiles, airplanes, houses with running water and central heat, churches, schools, stores, the clothes people wear, the food they eat, and the languages they speak.

And, in turn, if you could fly back in time to first-century A.D. Palestine, you would find yourself in a very different world from the world of today.

Yet, these two worlds have one important thing in common. Perhaps you can guess what it is—people. Two thousand years ago in Palestine there were boys and girls, just as there are today. These boys and girls asked some of the same questions you ask: How do I know what is true? What is God like? Is it always wrong to disobey? Why does this happen to me? Palestinian boys and girls liked adventures. They wanted to do important things. In fact, if you *could* talk to these boys or girls you might not find them strange even though their clothing, homes, and ideas might seem strange to you.

This book is about these boys and girls; that is, most of it is. The first story, "A Journey into Time," takes place in the present. It will tell you about Chuck and Ann and their twentieth-century adventures in Old Testament Jericho. As you visit Jericho with Chuck and Ann, you will discover how people today learn about life thousands of years ago.

Then you will move back through time, and in the other stories you will meet Jared and Martha and Juda and Benjamin and their families and friends. These are not true stories, but all the events in them might have happened. The places in which the stories occur are real places, and at the close of each story you will find more information about these places.

So, turn the page, meet Chuck and Ann, and—"journey into time."

A Journey into Time

A strange new country spread out before Chuck and Ann as they looked through the small window of the plane. By craning their necks they could see the snow-covered summit of Mount Hermon behind them. Almost directly below, the Jordan River squirmed its way between green banks. Beyond the green line of the river lay a vast expanse of brown desert.

"How much longer before we land?" Chuck asked his mother.

"Another twenty minutes and we should be in Amman," Mrs. Williams replied.

Ann wondered if her mother were as excited as she was. Here they were in Palestine! Here they were going to live for a whole month while their archeologist father continued his work at Old Testament Jericho. She and her brother would actually see and touch and even smell the country where Jesus had lived and taught.

The twin-engine plane bumped a little as it met the hot air rising from the Jordan Valley. Then, a few minutes later, the children saw the countryside more clearly, and they knew their long flight from the United States was about over.

As Ann stepped through the plane door, her first impression was one of walking straight into an oven. "Goodness, it's hot!" she exclaimed. Then she forgot the heat. "There's Dad," she cried.

Mrs. Williams, Ann, and Chuck ran down the steps of the plane toward the man who was waiting behind one of the airport gates.

"Hello! You're a welcome sight," he greeted them. "I'll be with you as soon as you've cleared customs and immigration. I have a car waiting outside to take us to Jericho."

"When will we get to the dig?" Chuck asked a little later as he and his sister and mother joined Mr. Williams in the airport lounge.

"Soon," his father promised. "It's not a long drive from here."

The car started out over the smooth road. As they left Amman behind, the scene changed from a busy city to the brown desert Ann had glimpsed from the plane. In the distance she noticed a few black tents. "Shepherds," her father explained.

For some minutes Ann looked at the desert landscape. Some of her enthusiasm began to subside. What would the next month be like? What would she and her brother do? Would they find any friends? How would she talk to people who spoke a different language from her own? A month was a long time to be lonely, and this countryside looked very lonely.

Mr. Williams seemed to sense her thoughts. "Jericho is very different from this desert," he remarked. "There are people there, even some Americans, and trees and flowers. Don't make up your mind about what the place is like until you've been here a little longer."

Ann laughed. "OK, I'll wait."

"We're almost there," Mr. Williams said sometime later. "Look." Chuck and Ann followed the direction of his pointing finger. They could make out the white walls of buildings, green trees and shrubs, and brilliantly colored flowers.

"We'll go directly to the house I've rented for your visit. Then, while you're getting settled, I'll see how things are at the dig."

"Let me go with you," Chuck pleaded.

"I think you'd better help with the unpacking first. I won't be long, and perhaps we can all visit the dig before the afternoon is over."

"When you go, Chuck, I go," Ann declared. "I've waited just as long as you have to see what an excavation is like."

"Aw, unpacking is woman's work," Chuck retorted.

When the car stopped before a small white house with a flat roof and thick walls, both children were too curious to pursue their argument. Inside the house it was dark and cool. It didn't take long to unload the suitcases, and then Mr. Williams left for the dig headquarters.

Chuck and Ann and Mrs. Williams explored the house and decided they would be very comfortable.

"Now let's see the town," Chuck suggested.

"All right," his mother agreed.

"Where's the dig?" Ann asked. "Isn't it right here?"

"No," Mrs. Williams replied. "It's over on the other side of the main road."

"But I thought it was in Jericho," Ann protested.

"It is and it isn't," her mother explained. "You see, there are really many Jerichos. There is this city where people live today. There is the Old Testament city which is many cities, how many the archeologists are trying to find out. And then there is the New Testament city some distance away."

"Many Jerichos!" Chuck exclaimed. "Is it like Los Angeles? You know, the Spanish city, and now the big city where we live?"

"Well, not exactly," his mother answered. "You'll find out a little later. I'm not going to try to tell you about it now because I think you'll understand better when you see for yourselves. There's nothing quite like it. You may be disappointed, but I think you'll be interested. Now, let's see what the Jericho of today has to show us."

Chuck and Ann found the next hour full of surprises. They saw a hotel which looked very modern and attractive, with its garden and flowers. Cars moved along the streets, and people in the same kind of clothes Americans wear seemed to be everywhere. But mingling with

these men and women in familiar dress were others in flowing robes like those Chuck and Ann had seen in pictures of Bible times. Women carried clay jugs on their heads. Some donkeys moved along heavily laden with household articles, grain, baskets, and food.

"The moving vans of the East," Chuck said as he watched the animals plod by.

Suddenly a boy about their own age approached them.

"Will you talk to me?" he asked. "I want to practice my English."

"You're learning English!" Chuck exclaimed.

"I learn to talk and write English," the boy replied.

Mrs. Williams laughed at the surprised look on her children's faces and then said to the boy, "We'll be glad to talk English with you."

When the boy wandered away a few minutes later, Ann said, "Well, at least one problem is solved. People here want to speak English to us. We won't have to learn Arabic in a month."

The Dig

"Is everyone ready?" Mr. Williams asked as he entered the house later that afternoon. Chuck and Ann ran to meet him.

"We've been waiting for hours!" they declared.

"All of fifteen minutes," Mrs. Williams added.

"Got your dark glasses? Good. You'll need them."

As the family walked along in the late afternoon sun, Mr. Williams explained about his work. "Remember," he said, "we're using the trench type of excavation, because we want to find out how many towns and cities were built on the place we're excavating. Another kind of excavation uncovers a whole area, perhaps an entire city. That kind is used at Khirbet Qumran near here."

"What do you mean by a trench?" Chuck asked. "A ditch?"

"I suppose you might call it that," Mr. Williams agreed. "But you'll soon see for yourself."

"There's the highway!" Ann exclaimed. "Now where's the dig?"

"Directly across it," her father answered, pointing to a mound of land which rose like a low hill on the other side of the road. "That's *Tell es-Sultân,* as Old Testament Jericho is known around here."

The group looked at the oval-shaped mound outlined against the brown foothills of the mountains of Judah. The mound appeared very small to be so famous. It was not much more than a few city blocks in length. No walls or buildings were visible, but as the party came nearer they saw robed Arab workmen carrying loads of dirt across the face of the slope to a dump on one side. Then they noticed people in western dress who were busy at different jobs. Chuck and Ann couldn't figure out what these people were doing.

"But where *is* Jericho?" Chuck asked. "I don't see *anything!*"

"You will when you look with the eyes of an archeologist," Mr. Williams assured him. "Come over this way."

11

Chuck and Ann followed their father, stepping carefully across the dirt, trying to keep out of the way of the working people.

"Let's stop here for a minute," Mr. Williams continued. "Look and tell me what you see."

Chuck and Ann studied the place before them. It was not very exciting. There was a rectangular area about the size of a small bathroom. Around it rose a low wall of crumbling mud brick. The area was marked by curious lines, looking like the marks of a braided rug that someone had pressed into soft mud and then removed.

· "Well," Chuck began. "It looks as though someone had tried to make a pattern in mud and then given up."

"That's a good try for a start, son. What you see is a room in which people lived seven or eight thousand years ago."

"Seven or eight thousand years!" Ann exclaimed. "That's a long time ago!"

"It certainly is," her father agreed. "The mud bricks are all that remain of the walls," he went on. "The marks in the floor tell us an interesting thing about the people who once lived here. They tried to make their homes comfortable and attractive just as we do now. Those peculiar marks are the impression of a rush mat that some woman made for her home. The mat has long since disappeared, but we know about it because it left its marks on the mud floor.

"We've learned other things about these homes. The people finished their walls and floors with their own brand of plaster. They raised grain and stored it in bins. Those who did all this couldn't read or write, but still they were able to work out ways of providing food and shelter for themselves and their families."

"Is the Old Testament eight thousand years old too?" Ann asked.

"No, Ann, it isn't as old as this ancient city. As a matter of fact, there were many cities here before the one that Joshua captured. Because a water supply was close, this was a good place to live.

12

So towns arose and were destroyed by war or some other disaster, and then new ones were built on top of the old. The practice of constructing one town on top of another gradually produced this mound. The Arabs call such a mound a *tell,* or man-made hill.

"But this is enough archeology for one day. I want you to meet someone. Mahmud!"

"Hello!" a voice responded.

Chuck and Ann looked around, but they couldn't see the person who spoke.

"Come up here," Mr. Williams called again.

"Right now," replied the voice.

The head and shoulders of a boy about Chuck's age popped up from the ground. His body and legs soon followed.

"Mahmud, here are Chuck and Ann, my son and daughter. This is Mahmud. His father works on the dig. Mahmud is quite a digger himself. And he has offered to be your official guide."

"Where were you when you spoke?" Chuck asked.

"In the trench over there," Mahmud pointed.

"You speak English!" Ann exclaimed.

"All my family does," Mahmud said proudly. "And some French."

Ann shook her head. "I feel stupid. I can only speak English."

Mahmud and Chuck were already walking toward the trench. When Ann caught up with them and looked down, she felt dizzy. "It's as deep as a well, a well that's long and not round! You go down there?"

"Sure," Mahmud replied. "We carried out all that dirt so your father can look at the sides of the trench. He's very smart. He can tell where each city stopped and a new one began! It's exciting!"

"Yes, I guess it is," Ann said doubtfully. "But I didn't know it was like this. I thought you found houses with roofs on top and skeletons, and oh, gold and other things."

"You are interested in skeletons? I'll show you some!"

"Great!" Chuck responded. "You really mean there are some around here?"

Ann shuddered. "I don't think I want to see them."

"Tomorrow I show you skeletons," Mahmud promised. "Now it's time for dinner. I must go."

He raced off, leaving Chuck and Ann standing by the trench where their father found them a few minutes later.

"Learn anything?" he asked.

"Yes," Ann replied. "But I didn't know it was so complicated. I thought you found things just the way they used to be. I don't see how you learn much from floors and trenches."

"It takes time and careful study and lots of experience," Mr. Williams told his daughter. "And you two can't learn all about it in one day. Let's get some dinner now. This evening I must work in the shed where we sort the pottery we find. Tomorrow we can return to the dig."

"Mahmud promised to show us some skeletons," Chuck said. "Does he really know where there are some?"

"He does," Mr. Williams assured him. "But you'll have to wait until tomorrow. There are no electric lights in ancient Jericho."

14

Tombs and People

Mahmud was waiting for Chuck and Ann the next morning. "To-day we go to the cemetery," he announced. "There is excitement there. New tombs are being found. Come." Mahmud started off toward the northern section of the excavation.

Ann dragged her feet a little as the boys hurried along. She wasn't sure she wanted to see any skeletons, but neither did she want to miss anything. When the three finally stopped, they were beyond the *tell* and on the edge of a community of small houses. To Ann's surprise and consternation, the workmen were digging in a tiny backyard.

"People live here!" she exclaimed.

"Right in the cemetery," Mahmud agreed. "But the cemetery is very old, and the people want us to find something. They get paid for what is found, and everyone feels very good."

Ann wasn't at all certain that she liked this until she thought how exciting it would be to find an ancient tomb in her own back yard. Then she joined the others who were waiting expectantly.

A hole had been opened up in the earth. Slowly and carefully the men cut down foot by foot into the dirt. What would they find? Who had dug this tomb originally? And how long ago? Ann wondered. Who was buried here?

At last the tomb entrance was cleared and one of the archeologists flashed a light into the chamber. Ann took a deep breath, then looked. There, resting peacefully, was the skeleton of a man. Later Ann learned he had been a tall man and old when he died, for most of his teeth were gone. By his side was a dagger.

Ann watched while the staff photographer took pictures, and she listened to the conversation of the archeologists. She had heard about people burying articles in tombs. Now she understood why tombs were important discoveries. Since the people believed they would live after death, they buried with each person the articles he had used so that he would have them in his next life.

"You never know what will show up," Ann heard a voice beside her say. She turned and saw one of the archeologists. "That's what makes our work so interesting," he went on. "You keep at it for days and days and don't find anything. Then something like this happens. It's a constant treasure hunt! How do you like this business of riding on a pick and shovel into the past?"

"I like it!" Ann told him earnestly. "But it's a little sad, too. I wonder who the man was."

"We'll probably never know, since the people didn't use headstones in those days."

"It takes a lot of work to find out about the past, doesn't it?" Ann remarked.

"It is hard work. The history books often forget to mention the sand that is swallowed, the heat and cold of the dig, and the flies that get in your food. But the books also forget to mention how exciting it is to be in on a new discovery. So I guess it evens up. But you know, the excavation isn't the most important part of our work."

"It isn't!" Ann exclaimed.

"No," the archeologist told her. "The really important part comes when we put all our finds together, like a jigsaw puzzle, and realize we have become acquainted with a lost period in history or with a people we didn't know existed. Working with the past makes you appreciate the great story of the human race. But now you'll excuse me—I've got work to do."

Ann was silent as she joined Mahmud and her brother who had gone over to another spot where more digging was in progress. "I wish I had a time machine," she thought. "I wish I could live for a day with each of the people who once lived in Jericho. But I'm glad J can be in on all this. I'm glad I'm living now."

Qumran on the Dead Sea

"How would you like to visit another excavation?" Mr. Williams asked his family several days later. "Remember what I told you about the famous Isaiah scroll that was found in a cave near the Dead Sea? How would you like to go to Khirbet Qumran to see the place? I have permission to go and can take you with me—if you can spare the time from Jericho!"

Ann looked at her father in surprise, and then noticed the twinkle in his eye.

"Try and keep me home!" she responded.

"When do we start?" Chuck was just as eager.

"Tomorrow morning. We'll leave early and take a picnic lunch so we can spend the day."

The following morning the family started on the drive to Qumran. Before long the outline of the Dead Sea was clearly visible, and sometime later the tents of the Qumran excavation team appeared.

"This trip will give you a chance to see another type of dig," Mr. Williams explained. "At Khirbet Qumran the whole site is being cleared."

When the family got out of the car, they stopped for a moment to take in the view. Away to the north, the brown hills of Judah were visible. Behind them, to the west, was a line of sheer, desolate cliffs. Southward the Dead Sea merged into more cliffs and hills.

"What a barren place," Mrs. William exclaimed. "Imagine living all your life with only a few trees in sight and that salty sea in your front yard!"

Mr. Williams laughed. "But the people who lived here did a good job in building their community."

"What happened here?" Chuck asked.

"What people are you talking about?" added Ann, without waiting for her father to answer Chuck.

"All in time," their father teased. "And now that you're getting pretty good at using your archeologist's eyes, let's take a look."

The group walked over to where the outlines of a large structure were visible. "The people who built this community were very religious Jewish men," Mr. Williams said. "This was probably the central building." He pointed to one section and explained that it may have served as a kitchen for the entire community. Toward the east, closer to the Dead Sea, a large hall had once stood.

"Here the excavation team found a real mystery. In their digging the workers discovered many strangely shaped plaster fragments which no one could identify. The fragments were collected and sent to the Palestine Museum in Jerusalem. When the pieces were fitted together they turned out to be a long narrow table, a bench, and a low platform. But what were these used for? Then, a little later, in the same area, two inkwells were found. One even contained some dried ink. The mystery was solved. The room above this was the writing room where manuscripts were copied. When the floor caved in, the table and bench and platform fell into the room below and were broken."

"What manuscripts?" Chuck asked.

Mr. Williams grinned. "You should be able to answer that one for yourself."

"I know," Ann exclaimed. "The Dead Sea scrolls!"

"So it is thought," Mr. Williams answered.

"But where were they found?" Chuck asked.

"We have enough time to climb up there before lunch. Want to?" his father asked.

"You bet!"

Ann and her mother, Chuck and Mr. Williams left the excavation and began a hot climb up the side of one of the cliffs. It was hard work. Before they had gone very far, Chuck was thinking of the thermos jug of cold water in the car. He wondered if the people who had lived in this community and hidden the scrolls had been thirsty and hot.

"How much farther?" Ann gasped.

"We're almost there," Mr. Williams encouraged her.

"But I don't see anything."

"Neither did a lot of other people for a long time," Mr. Williams responded.

"There's the cave," Chuck shouted suddenly as he scrambled up the last few feet to a dark hole in the side of the cliff.

One by one they slipped through the cave opening to find themselves inside a rocky chamber. Mr. Williams threw the beam of his flashlight around the cave.

"I wonder how the people felt who found the manuscripts," Ann remarked.

"Scared at first," Mr. Williams told her.

"How exactly were they found?" Chuck asked.

"Purely by accident," his father replied. "The story is that a shep-

19

herd was roaming around these cliffs looking for a lost sheep. He tossed a stone as people sometimes do. The stone went through a hole, and made a strange sound as if it had broken something. The fellow must have been frightened, because he went for help before he investigated. A little later he returned with a friend. Together they explored the cave and found broken pottery jars and the manuscripts which had been stored in the jars. One of them was the famous Isaiah scroll."

"I wonder how many other manuscripts are still hidden in caves

20

in these cliffs," Ann mused. "Wouldn't it be exciting to find some ourselves!"

"Exciting, yes, but highly unlikely," Mr. Williams told her. "For a number of years these cliffs have been searched with just this hope in mind. And I don't really recommend starting on such a treasure hunt. It's hot, tiring, and usually unfruitful work. I'm ready for another kind of treasure right now—lunch!"

"I'm with you on that," Chuck declared. "Let's see if we can make it back faster than we came up."

The climb down was easier, but Ann thought that if everyone carried away as much sand in his shoes as she did, the cliffs wouldn't last another thousand years.

After lunch the group wandered around the Qumran excavation for an hour or so before starting the trip back to Jericho.

"Archeologists don't make all the discoveries," Chuck observed. "That shepherd did pretty well with his find!"

"Yes, archeologists don't make all the discoveries," Mr. Williams agreed. "But without their help, we wouldn't know when the Isaiah manuscript was written or by whom."

"Or where!" Ann stated. "Imagine finding the writing table and the ink! I'll bet there are lots of things still to be found around here. Dad, I wish we didn't have to go home. I wish you could go on digging."

"It doesn't happen as easily as that, Ann. It takes money and planning and lots of thinking before an expedition can dig. But there's another good reason for stopping our work soon. Summer will be here before long, and then it really will be hot. But there'll be other years and other excavations. As long as there are secrets to be uncovered, there will be men and women eager and willing to uncover them."

"One thing, sure, we're going to have lots to talk about when we get home," Chuck remarked.

"And that time is coming soon," Mrs. Williams added.

Farewell

"Everyone is busy," Ann said sadly to her brother one morning. "Even Mahmud hasn't any time for us. I hate to see the work stop."

"Well, they have to quit some time. Let's go over to the dig for a last visit. Something may be happening. I'll tell Mother we're going."

Chuck found his mother busy with the family packing. "We're taking back a lot more than we brought," she remarked.

"That's because of Chuck's rocks," Ann teased.

Chuck laughed. "Well, people are going to like paperweights made from Jericho stones. I'm glad I thought of that. Maybe Joshua stepped on some of the rocks I'm carrying home. You never can tell."

"No, you certainly can't," his mother agreed. "But how would you and Ann like a picnic supper tonight? I'll get some food ready, and we could eat out near the dig."

"Great!" Chuck replied. "May I invite Mahmud?"

"Of course."

As Chuck and Ann wandered over the dig they tried to make up stories about the people who had lived in the homes that had been uncovered.

When they reached the excavation they watched the preparations for closing up the work. "It's almost as much trouble to stop as to start," Ann observed.

"They want to leave everything in good condition so the work can be continued another year. Let's find Mahmud."

When Mahmud saw them approaching, he stopped what he was doing and beckoned to them. "Would you like a souvenir?" he asked.

"Sure," they replied.

"Look," he said, leading them over to a large box. Inside the box Ann saw a quantity of small black particles.

"What is it?" she asked.

"Grain," he replied. "Real grain that someone stored for food. But it never was used. There was a fire, I guess, and the grain was burned. But there it is. And before you leave you can have some to take home. I was told to tell you."

"This is a better souvenir than your rocks, Chuck," Ann exclaimed. "I wonder how old it is."

"Thousands of years," Mahmud replied.

"I'll just put a grain or two in my paperweights," Chuck declared. "Thanks, Mahmud. Oh, we came to ask you something. Will you go on a picnic with us this afternoon?"

"Sure," Mahmud replied. "I'll see you later."

As the shadows of the Judah hills spread across the Jericho *tell,* the Williams family and Mahmud left for the picnic. Walking westward they could see a brown hill rising directly in front of them. Part way up its side Chuck noticed a stone building that looked as though it had been pasted on the sheer slope.

"What's that?" Chuck pointed toward the building.

"That's a Greek monastery," Mr. Williams replied. "It was built there because tradition says this is the Mount of Temptation where Jesus went after his baptism."

"Did Jesus really climb that hill?" Ann asked with interest.

"We don't know," her father answered, "and we have no way of finding out. But sometime in the past it was called the Mount of Temptation, and we still call it that today."

"That's why you said, 'tradition says'?" Ann questioned.

"Right," Mr. Williams replied.

"Here is the country of the Bible all around us," Ann said to herself as she walked over the rocky ground. "And people lived here long before the Bible was written." She looked at the Mount of Temptation and wondered if Jesus really had climbed its side and stayed there in the brown, hot wilderness.

She looked toward the excavation where men and women were still working in the late afternoon. "Brothers and sisters played in those houses just as we play today," she thought. "Mothers cooked and fathers planted and harvested grain. I'll bet they even had picnics. People are not so very different today."

The sun was disappearing behind the hills as the family and Mahmud settled down for supper.

"Dad," Chuck said, "you haven't told us anything about the walls of Jericho in the story of Joshua. Isn't this the place?"

"This is the same site, Chuck," his father replied. "But the excavators ran into a piece of hard luck when they tried to find out about Joshua's time. See that road down there?"

"Sure," Chuck nodded. It was the highway he crossed every time he went from his home to the dig.

"Well, the famous wall fortifications of Joshua's time were largely destroyed by weather and by later inhabitants who used bricks and stones from the wall to build their homes. We haven't been able to find any traces of those walls. We think there may have been some remains in the area where that road was cut. But those who constructed the road destroyed whatever may have been left of the fortification without realizing what they were doing. At least no remains have turned up. But we do know something about the life of the Canaanite people Joshua conquered, and probably the life of the people is more important than the walls."

"I guess it is," Ann said thoughtfully. "That's what I've learned from being here—that the Bible is about real people."

"Yes," Mr. Williams said, "walking over this land and looking at the remains of the houses make the Bible real. And that's one of the purposes of the archeologist—to make the past real by finding out all we can about its people."

A soft breeze swept over the spot where the group sat, stirring the dust and moving the brown grass. Ann and Chuck and Mahmud were

silent. Ann looked toward the hills in the west and knew that over there was Jerusalem, and many miles farther away, her own home. In her imagination she could see the people who had lived in this valley for thousands of years and who had left behind so many reminders of their everyday life. Now these people were very much part of her own world. She thought again of the handful of grain she would take home with her and wondered once more about the family that had stored that grain. Had the children in that family ever sat where she was sitting? It made her rather uncomfortable, yet excited, to realize that perhaps they had. When she had started on her trip she knew she was going to another land. But she hadn't guessed she would also be making a journey back into time. She would never forget either journey.

The stars were clear in the night sky as the group packed up their picnic things and started toward the lights of modern Jericho. Tomorrow they would leave for Amman and the plane that would start them on their way home. Someday, Ann promised herself, she would return. Perhaps the time would come when she, too, could work on an excavation, helping to dig up the past.

MORE ABOUT JERICHO

The Jericho that Chuck and Ann visited is the site that was inhabited from before 6000 B.C., eight thousand years before anyone living today was born.

The Jericho of Jesus' time was a mile and three quarters to the south where another source of water made it possible for people to live. Here Herod the Great built a magnificent palace, and it was this city that Jesus had in mind when he told the story of the good Samaritan. Very few remains of this city exist.

Present-day Jericho is about a mile from the Old Testament location, but it uses the same water supply that Joshua's city used. Visitors to Jericho today are impressed by the beauty of the trees and shrubs, thriving in the midst of the hot, brown desert. Here tourists like to go in the winter months to escape the rain and cold of Jerusalem, for the average annual rainfall is only four inches a year, and the warm air is comfortable. But the summer months are hot and unpleasant.

You can read about Jericho in your Bible. Below are some references that will tell you more about what happened there in Bible times.

OLD TESTAMENT JERICHO

Do you remember the story of Moses who led the Israelites through the wilderness toward a new home in a new land where they would not be slaves as they had been in Egypt? Moses did not live long enough to enter this new land. He did, however, see it from the top of Mount Pisgah. As he looked across toward Canaan where his people would live, Jericho was directly before him. *Deuteronomy 34:1–8* tells what Moses saw. This passage also tells about his death and his burial in an unknown place.

Sometime later the Israelites did enter Jericho, with Joshua as their leader. Read about this event in *Joshua 6:1–20*. As you read, try to hear the sound of marching feet, the noise of the horns, and the excited shouts of the people.

NEW TESTAMENT JERICHO

We do not know how many times Jesus visited the Jericho of New Testament days, but we are sure that he knew this city fairly well. The familiar story of the good Samaritan in *Luke 10:29–37* helps us to understand how difficult and dangerous it was to travel from Jerusalem to Jericho. *Luke 19:1–10* tells about Jesus' experiences with a man who lived in Jericho.

A jar of grain several thousand years old, found in the Jericho dig.

A Jericho tomb. The skeleton is lying on a bed with its elbow resting on a table. Also in the tomb are baskets, pottery, a number of other skeletons, and remains of a large supply of food.

the Missing Coin

"There's Ahab!" Jared said crossly as he and his friend, Simon, turned the corner of one of the narrow streets of Nazareth.

"What does he have?" Simon asked.

"I don't know, and I don't care," Jared replied. "But he'll tell us all about it if it's something he thinks we don't have."

Farther down the street Ahab was tossing a brightly colored object into the air with one hand and catching it easily with the other.

"Hello," Ahab greeted the two as they approached.

"Hello," Jared answered coldly.

"Want to play? I have a new ball."

"No thanks, we're busy," Jared responded, but his eyes lingered on the ball Ahab was holding. Probably Ahab's father had bought it on his recent trip, for he was a merchant and one of the more prosperous men in Nazareth.

"Why did you say we were busy?" Simon questioned his friend as Ahab wandered away.

"Did you want to play with him?" Jared asked.

"No-o," Simon spoke slowly. "But I'd like to try that ball."

"You know what would have happened. Ahab would have told us what to play and how to play it and complained if we got a speck of dust on his beautiful new ball," Jared complained. "That's the way it always is when you play with him."

"I guess you're right," Simon replied, "but maybe we ought to play with him a little anyway."

"Oh, he'll get along. Let's see if we can find that cave you discovered yesterday. Father said he wouldn't need me this afternoon."

Simon agreed, and the two boys started up through the meadows that were bright with flowers from the winter rains. After they had climbed for a few minutes, they looked back over the valley. They could see the flat-roofed houses of Nazareth where they lived and the synagogue where they attended school. The caravan trail from Damascus, which wound around the foot of the hills on which Nazareth stood, was clearly visible in the distance.

"I wonder if we'll ever see Damascus," Simon remarked. "I think I'll be a merchant when I grow up and bring my camels loaded with silks and spices along that road."

"You'll probably be a coppersmith like your father, and I'll be a potter. Little chance we'll ever have to see the world."

"Well," Simon replied, "at least we'll see Jerusalem. Two months and we'll be on our way."

Jared forgot his grumpiness. "Just two months!"

The boys looked across the plain of Esdraelon to where the Jerusalem road emerged from the Samarian hills. In their minds they could see themselves walking southward along that road toward the holy city and the Passover celebration in the temple.

Suddenly a rabbit darted from the brush ahead, and they ran after it. But the rabbit was quicker and more at home in the heavy growth of the hillside. Simon and Jared soon gave up and climbed on until they found the cave.

It was pleasant under the overhanging rock, and the afternoon passed quickly while they talked of Jerusalem and their plans for the Passover journey.

In the days that followed, there was little time to dream of travel and adventure. Jared was kept busy helping his father, Obed, turn out the clay jugs and pots used by the women of Nazareth, and Simon worked hard on the copper utensils his father made. Mornings were spent in the synagogue school learning to read and write Hebrew. Although the boys had heard Hebrew all their lives in the synagogue service, it was almost a foreign language to them, for Aramaic was spoken among the people of Nazareth.

Jared and Simon found their studies hard. There were times when only the prodding of the rabbi kept them working. Ahab, to Jared's annoyance, was quick at his lessons, and there were many painful moments when the rabbi praised Ahab for his good memory and scolded Jared for his frequent mistakes.

"Why does he have to be so smart?" Jared muttered one morning when Ahab had recited a long passage from the law without a single error. "I'll bet he couldn't turn out a pot on my father's wheel."

One afternoon several days later Ahab came by the shop where Jared was busy helping his father finish an order for several bowls.

Ahab watched as Jared's fingers molded the soft clay on the wheel while his foot pushed rhythmically on the treadle that kept the wheel revolving. Jared pretended not to see him.

"Is that hard to do?" Ahab asked after several minutes.

"Harder than memorizing the law," Jared replied.

"Will you let me try it?" Ahab asked.

"Why should I?" Jared started to say. Then he thought, "I'll teach him a lesson."

"When I finish this bowl, if my father will let you," he said aloud.

Soon the sides of the bowl rose to their proper height as Jared guided

31

the clay. Then, quickly, he changed the position of his hands and formed the rim.

"There," Jared commented. "That's the last, Father," he called to the back of the shop. "Ahab wants to try the wheel. May he?"

"All right," Obed replied. "Then help me prepare this clay."

Ahab sat on the low stool and put his foot on the treadle as Jared had done. Jared picked up a lump of clay and slapped it against the wooden bench that held the finished bowls. Then he placed the clay on the wheel and showed Ahab how to hold his hands. But when Ahab tried to move his foot up and down while keeping his fingers steady around the soft clay, he got into trouble. A queer, lopsided dish was the best he could produce.

"Pretty good for a beginner," Ahab declared. "With some practice I'll bet I could turn out a jug like that!" Ahab pointed to a large water pot standing in the doorway of the shop.

"Anything you'd make would never sell in the Nazareth market," Jared responded angrily. "You're lucky you don't have to earn your food with your hands and feet."

"Well, I don't." Ahab spoke sharply. "I'm going to be a merchant like my father when I grow up. And I won't sell your pots. You can depend on that!"

"Don't worry—you won't have the chance," Jared shouted as Ahab ran off down the street.

At sundown both Jared and his father were tired and glad to put their work away. They washed the soft brown clay from their hands and walked across the courtyard that separated the shop from their house. As they entered they touched the mezuzah on the doorpost. Jared was glad to be greeted by the good smells of the evening meal.

When the food was ready, Obed bowed his head. "Bless thou this food, O Lord God of the universe," he prayed. "May it strengthen us in body as we try to fulfill thy holy law in our daily lives. Amen."

Midway through the meal, Obed exclaimed, "How could I forget! Saul paid me this morning for the pots I made for his daughter's new home, and I left the coin in the shop. Jared, run and get it. The coin is in the small bowl at the end of the shelf."

Jared ran back to the shop and looked on the shelf. He saw the small bowl, but it was lying on its side. When he turned it over to let the coin fall out, there was no coin. Anxiously Jared looked around. He examined every article on the shelf. He crawled over the floor and ran his fingers along the ground beneath the bench that stood below the shelf. The coin was gone. Perhaps his father had forgotten where he put it.

As Jared was taking another look all around the shop Obed's voice interrupted him. "What's keeping you so long? Where is the coin?"

"I can't find it, Father."

"Can't find it—where's the bowl I told you to look for?"

"Here, Father, but it had turned over, and I thought the coin might have rolled out."

Together the two searched every inch of the shop before they finally gave up.

"Somebody must have seen me hiding the coin and taken it while we were working on the clay. Who was here this afternoon?"

"Ahab was—but I know he didn't take it. I watched him every minute. And the customers. But you saw them."

"We need that money," Obed said angrily. "It would have paid for a good part of our trip this spring. Someone waited for the opportunity and walked off with it."

Jared looked at his father with concern. "Does this mean we can't go to Jerusalem?"

"I hope not, but it will make the trip harder to manage. We'd better tell your mother."

Jared's mother had already guessed that something was wrong. "What kept you so long?" she asked.

"The coin is gone," Obed told her. "It was taken while Jared and I were working on new clay. I was foolish to leave it where I did, but I've never lost money before. We'll have to ask and see if anyone knows about the coin."

The next day Obed questioned neighbors and friends. Everyone showed concern, but no one had any information about what had become of the money.

The mystery of the missing coin puzzled Jared in the days that followed. But it was temporarily forgotten one afternoon when Jared's cousin, Joshua, stopped in the shop.

"Greetings, Obed," Joshua said. "I've come to see if I can borrow your son for a day or so."

"Borrow Jared?" Obed asked. "What do you mean?"

"The day after tomorrow I'm taking the sheep back into the hills, and I need a few boys to help me. I thought Jared and Simon might welcome a chance to see the summer pasture. Simon's father says he can go if Jared has your permission. What do you say?"

"Oh, Father, please," Jared begged.

"Well, I guess I can spare you." Obed answered. "But you'll have to make up your lessons."

Joshua rumpled Jared's hair. "Good. You'll get a taste of shepherd life. I'm going to ask Ahab, too. You three ought to make a good team."

"Ahab!" Jared's face fell. "Why does he have to go?"

"Why, Jared! Don't you want him?" Joshua asked.

"No!" Jared said emphatically. "He's always bragging about the trips he makes with his father and about how good he is at everything. I don't think I want to go if he's along."

"I'm surprised," Joshua said. "I thought you and Ahab were friends!"

"No, I don't want him for a friend."

"Maybe he wants you."

"He has a funny way of showing it," Jared muttered.

"Sometimes people do that because they don't know any other way to try to be a friend." Joshua regarded Jared thoughtfully and then said, "All right, I won't ask Ahab. I'll see you day after tomorrow."

Herding Sheep with Joshua

Two mornings later the sun was just rising above the hills to the east of Nazareth when a noisy party moved slowly away from the village. Through the winter the sheep had been pastured in the meadows nearby, but now it was time to take them farther back into the hills where they would join other flocks in the summer pasture lands. Jared and Simon were sure the animals didn't want to be moved. They bleated and resisted the prodding of the men and boys who urged them along.

Throughout the day progress was slow. Several times Jared was certain the flock intended to stay where it was. But gradually the familiar landscape of Nazareth vanished from sight, and the boys found themselves in new country. They saw inviting caves and clear streams, but they were too busy to explore or to cool their tired feet.

That night Jared and Simon lay down under the stars. In the distance they heard the howling of wolves, but none came near the camp. Jared's eyes searched the night sky. The stars were the same as those he saw from the rooftop of his home in Nazareth. "Stars don't change," he thought, stretching his tired legs. "These are the same stars King David knew when he was a shepherd. I wonder how God made the stars. I wonder where the sky ends." Then he fell asleep.

It was Simon who nudged him awake the next morning. "Get up. We're moving."

Jared looked around. The men were busy among the flock although the sun had not yet appeared. His back ached from sleeping on the bumpy ground, and his muscles hurt when he stood up.

"I don't think I can walk," he complained.

"Well, you'd better. Your camel isn't here this morning."

Jared laughed at the thought of herding sheep from a camel's back.

"Here's your breakfast," Simon continued, handing him some dried fruit and bread. "We can get a drink in that stream over there."

Jared took the food and ate it as he followed Simon toward the stream. He bathed his feet and ducked his head in the cold water.

"Simon, Jared, we need you over here," Joshua called. "Get those animals to follow the others. We have a distance to travel today if we're to make the pasture before sundown."

The two boys ran to the edge of the flock where a few sheep were insisting on a long breakfast before they began their journey. With much urging they were persuaded to join the rest, and another day's work began.

Jared wondered what Ahab was doing. "Probably learning his lessons so he can show me up when I get back," he said to himself. "But he's never been a shepherd. I wish we'd meet a wolf. I'd take his tail back and wave it in Ahab's face."

It was almost dark when Joshua came with the good news that their destination lay just ahead. "You'll spend the night with us, and tomorrow you two and one of the men who is not staying with the flock will go back. You should be able to make the return trip easily in one day."

Jared and Simon were too tired to care.

Joshua grinned at them. "Do you think you want to be shepherds when you grow up?"

"No," Jared said wearily. "I'm going to be a potter. I've never walked so far in my whole life as I did chasing those sheep. Why are you a shepherd, Joshua?"

"Because I like it," Joshua replied. "I like knowing that the sheep need me, and I like being outdoors. It's a good life and important work."

"I guess it is," Jared agreed. "And I'm glad you like it." Then he realized Joshua might think him ungrateful. "Thank you for inviting me to come with you. But I don't think I could spend my whole summer away from my family and friends."

"It is a lonely life, Jared. But shepherds have the companionship of one another, and out here on the hills we have time to think about the wisdom of God who made us and the world we live in."

Jared was silent for a moment, thinking. "But I don't believe that God wants me to be a shepherd," he said slowly. "I'm going to make things with my hands." He looked at his brown hands and remembered how good the moist clay felt as he made it take whatever shape he wished.

"We must all find the thing we can do well and be happy when others do the same. But right now you need food and rest. Sleep well."

The trip home was not hard. Jared and Simon were surprised to see the houses of Nazareth come into view while the sun was still high in the sky. Sheep were even slower than they had realized.

As Jared approached his home his thoughts returned to the trip to Jerusalem and that strangely missing coin. Who had it? Or was it still somewhere around? Jared wondered if he would ever know.

Almost a Man

After school the following day Jared and Simon looked around for Ahab, but he was nowhere in sight. "He doesn't want to see us now that we have something to tell him," Jared said crossly. "Oh well, let him wonder what we did."

Simon didn't seem to care. His mind was full of plans for the journey to Jerusalem, now but a week away. "Jared, what will the temple be like? My father says there's nothing like it in the whole world."

"We'll soon be able to see for ourselves, and then when we come back we'll be joining the men in the synagogue."

Suddenly the importance of this became real to Jared as it never had before. All his life he had joined the women and children in the gallery of the synagogue. In another week he would be thirteen and no longer required to sit with the women. He would be a man of Israel!

The next day was Friday, always a busy time in Jared's home. His mother prepared the food that her family would need for the sabbath so she would not have to work and break the fourth commandment. Clothing was mended because it was against the law to take more than two stitches on the sabbath. Their little home was thoroughly cleaned.

At sundown the sabbath lamp was lighted, and special prayers were said before the evening meal. Jared always looked forward to the sabbath, when the family wore its best clothes and ate the best meal of the week, but this sabbath he regarded with particular anticipation and seriousness. It was his last sabbath as a boy—seven days from now he would be a man.

On the sabbath morning the family went to the synagogue. His father left the others as they approached the main court. He washed his hands in a basin provided for this purpose. Then he entered the main door, which faced Jerusalem, and joined the men. Jared and the others went around to the rear where they climbed to the gallery. From his seat Jared looked down on the congregation of men. He saw the ark in the front of the synagogue where the sacred scripture was kept and the low seats just below the ark where the leaders sat.

He waited as the ruler of the synagogue stood and counted the men. More than ten were present, the number required before a service could be held. Jared imagined himself sitting with the men, with the ruler's eyes on him, counting him as one who was present.

Then the rabbi rose and stepped to the reader's desk. He and the men began to chant, "Hear, O Israel: the LORD our God is one LORD; and you shall love the LORD your God with all your heart, and with all your soul, and with all your might."

Jared listened to the deep voices of the men. Soon he would be speaking with them, declaring his love for the God of his people.

The ruler of the synagogue took a roll of the law from the ark and handed it to his assistant who gave it to the rabbi. The rabbi opened the metal case and reverently kissed the silken cloth that covered the roll. Then he carefully unrolled the parchment scroll. Jared listened intently as the rabbi began to read the great laws that Moses had received from the Lord.

"I am the LORD your God, who brought you out of the land of Egypt, out of the house of bondage.

"You shall have no other gods before me."

Jared knew these words. He had heard them often in his home. Now, as he listened, he thought of Moses and the other leaders of his people. It seemed to Jared that God was speaking to him now as he listened to the rabbi's words.

"You shall not steal.

"You shall not bear false witness against your neighbor."

Jared looked across the gallery toward Simon who was gazing steadily at the rabbi. Then Jared noticed Ahab who was also watching with great seriousness. Suddenly, Jared realized that Ahab, too, was about to become a man of Israel. And Ahab knew the law far better than he, Jared,

did. But today Ahab listened as though he were hearing the rabbi's words for the first time.

"You shall not covet—"

Jared again glanced in Ahab's direction and their eyes met. What was Ahab thinking? "You shall not covet." Jared pushed the thought away from him. He knew he had been guilty of wanting the things Ahab possessed. Jared was very uncomfortable.

When the rabbi finished reading, he returned the scroll to the ruler's assistant and began to speak.

"Today there are with us several boys who will soon join our congregation as men. In their homes they have heard the stories of the great leaders of our people who were sent by God to help us know his will. These boys have been taught the law and the prophets. But to know the law is not enough. The true man of Israel is the one who practices it in all his relationships with others, because he loves God and chooses above everything else to obey his will. Men of Israel, and you who are about to become men, be obedient, for these commandments of Moses are ties that bind us to one another and to the Lord our God, who did not forsake us in the past and will not forsake us today."

The rabbi bowed his head and led the congregation in prayer.

As Jared left the synagogue with his mother, she put her hand on his arm. "You're growing up, my son. When you return from Jerusalem, you will no longer sit with me, and I shall be proud as I see you below with the men. I know you will be a good Jew and a good man."

Jared nodded. "I want to be. I hope God will help me to be."

Two Discoveries

When Jared returned from the synagogue school the next day, he went to his father's shop. To his surprise, a neighbor was there.

"Where's Father?" Jared asked.

"He's home," the neighbor replied. "I'm sorry, Jared."

"Sorry?" Jared asked in surprise. "Why?"

"You'd better go home," the neighbor said kindly.

Jared was troubled. What had happened? He rushed across the court-yard toward his house.

As he burst through the door, his father came to meet him. "Quiet, Jared. Your mother is sick."

"But she was all right this morning," Jared exclaimed.

"She wasn't feeling too well when you left and grew worse during the morning. I didn't call you from school because there's nothing to worry about. But she needs rest. Go back to the shop and tell my friend that you will stay there during the afternoon. I'll join you as soon as I can leave your mother."

Jared went out slowly. What had happened to his mother? Was she very sick?

The afternoon wore on. Jared worked at the wheel for a while. Then he decided he'd have another look for the coin. He turned each piece of pottery upside down and shook it, but there was no tinkle of metal on the hard floor. At last he gave up and settled down to wait for his father.

At sundown Obed appeared. "Your mother is sleeping, and we will close the shop now. I see you've been rearranging things."

"No, Father. Just searching. I thought I might find the lost coin. You'll need it for medicine now that Mother is ill."

"I wish you could find it, Jared, but I'm afraid that money is gone forever. Come home now. You've done a good day's work."

The next morning Jared's mother was no better. In two days the group from Nazareth would be leaving for Jerusalem. A new worry entered Jared's mind. Surely he would be able to go. He must go. But the following day, when Jared looked at his mother, he knew his father would not be able to leave her.

Jared sat on the doorstep of his home and threw pebbles into the courtyard. Concern for his mother and disappointment over what her illness had done to his plans made him miserable. Why did this have to happen? For many months he had looked forward to seeing the temple in Jerusalem and to celebrating the Passover there. Simon was going. Ahab was going. But he would be left at home.

"It's not fair, God," he thought to himself. "Now Ahab will brag about all he sees, and even Simon will boast about his adventures."

"Greetings, Jared!" Jared looked up startled and saw Ahab coming toward him.

"What do you want?" he asked with some annoyance.

Then he noticed Ahab's father also entering the courtyard.

"I've brought you something, and we've come to ask you something. And I'm sorry your mother is ill."

Ahab held out his hand. In it was a silver coin stuck in a piece of brown clay.

"Where did you get that!" Jared exclaimed.

"Remember the bowl I made on the wheel? Yesterday I knocked it on the floor and broke it. I was sorry because it's the only thing I've ever made, but when I picked up the pieces, I found this in the clay."

"The coin! My father's coin!"

Obed came to the door. "Welcome," he greeted the visitors.

"Look, Father! Ahab found your coin. But I don't see how it got into the clay."

"You must have caught it in the clay when you threw it around before you gave it to me," Ahab suggested.

Jared was ashamed. "I guess I was showing off. Thanks, Ahab."

"This will be useful now," Obed said as he took the coin. "I'm grateful to you for returning it."

Ahab smiled. "My father wants to know if Jared may go with us to Jerusalem."

"The trip means a lot to my son," Ahab's father explained. "And I know Jared must have counted on it. We'd be glad to have him travel with us."

"Oh, Father, may I?" Jared asked eagerly.

Obed spoke slowly. "Yes, you may. I had hoped to be with you when you saw the temple for the first time, but it isn't fair to keep you home, and I cannot leave."

Jared looked at his father and noticed how tired and worried he was. "If I go, my father will have no one to watch the shop for him, and I won't know how my mother is," he thought.

"Thank you very much," Jared said to Ahab and his father. "I'd like to go, but I'm needed here."

Ahab's father turned to Obed. "We're sorry Jared can't make the trip, but you can be proud of your son. He is already a man. Will you tell your wife we wish her a quick recovery?"

As they turned to leave Jared stopped Ahab. "When you get back, you can make another bowl—and will you tell me about Jerusalem?"

"Sure," Ahab promised. "And thanks!"

As Jared went into the house with his father, he wasn't altogether happy. He wanted so much to see Jerusalem. His father seemed to understand. "We'll go next year," he promised. "We will go together."

MORE ABOUT NAZARETH

Nazareth was a small village in Jared's time, but it was not isolated from the rest of the world. Caravans from Damascus passed near the town, and the main road running south to Jerusalem and Egypt was not far to the west. So Jared and his family knew what was happening in the world, as did Jesus and his family.

The people of Nazareth made their living in a number of ways. There was undoubtedly a village potter and a coppersmith, and a village carpenter. Many families were farmers, cultivating the hillsides that were covered with fields of grain, vineyards, and olive orchards. On their hikes among the Nazareth hills, boys like Jared and Simon would have seen farmers taking grapes and vegetables on heavily laden donkeys to sell in the communities nearby.

Today Nazareth is still rather small, but it is famous as the place where Jesus grew up. It lies on a slope in the Galilean hills at an altitude of about 1,100 feet. Many modern houses and other buildings may be seen by tourists, but there are also some narrow streets with open shops very similar to those of Jesus' day. And the people of the village still get their water from the spring that supplied the well used in the first century A.D.

Jesus lived in Nazareth until he was about thirty years old, and it was from Nazareth that he made his first trip to Jerusalem when he was twelve. You can read about this trip and his unexpected disappearance in *Luke 2:41–52*.

We don't know how many times Jesus revisited Nazareth after his baptism, but in *Luke 4:16–22* we learn of one occasion. As you read this passage, try to imagine yourself in the synagogue congregation, hearing Jesus speak, trying to understand the meaning of his words. What would you think about him if you were among those who listened?

An old street in present-day Nazareth. The streets of Jesus' day were probably narrow like this one.

the Strange Guest

Back and forth, back and forth Martha bent to the rhythm of the circling mill. It always gave her pleasure to see the white flour pouring out from between the two round stones as the grain was ground fine and smooth.

"Soon there will be enough," Ruth told her daughter. Martha was glad, because today her arms were tired and her shoulders ached. For a longer time than usual she and her mother had been working in the courtyard of their home, preparing extra flour for the meals of the Hanukkah feast.

Suddenly Martha saw a shadow fall across the mill. It was not the leafy pattern of the olive tree growing in a corner of the courtyard, but a heavy shadow that passed quickly and was gone.

Martha looked up and gasped with fright. Her mother exclaimed, "A Roman soldier!"

They saw the man just as he slipped through the open doorway of their home.

48

"There's something wrong with him. He can hardly walk. Mother, what will he do?"

Ruth's face was very troubled. The two were alone at their home on the outskirts of Bethlehem, for Martha's father, Ruben, had left many hours before to work in the fields and olive orchard.

"Mother, let's go for help. He may kill us!"

Ruth rose quickly. "Going for help might bring more trouble," she told her daughter. "If the Romans are searching the homes of our village, we can't do much to stop them. I'll find out what he wants."

"Don't go in the house," Martha pleaded.

"You stay out here," Ruth directed. "And if I don't come out in a few minutes, run to Asa's and tell him what has happened."

Martha watched fearfully as her mother entered the small white house.

At first Ruth could see little. The house was dark and cool after the bright glare of the sun in the courtyard. Then she noticed the man leaning against one of the walls as if seeking support. He was watching her closely.

"Please listen to me," he begged, before Ruth could say anything. "I won't harm you. I need help."

"What are you doing here?" Ruth asked. "We've paid our taxes. We have nothing to hide."

"Please listen," the man repeated. "I've run away from the army. I do need help."

Ruth's first impulse was to hurry outside. If this man were a deserter from the Roman army, hiding him was dangerous. Her husband could be imprisoned or killed for it. Then she looked at the man again and saw that his left arm was held against his side in a rough sling. Blood stained the sleeve of his tunic, which was soiled and torn.

"What has happened to you? What do you want?" Ruth asked cautiously.

49

"Mother, are you all right?" Martha called from the courtyard.

"Yes, dear. But stay near the gate. I'm going to find out what the soldier wants."

The young man, for now Ruth could see that he was not more than eighteen or nineteen, took a step forward, then fell.

"I'm sorry," he said as he tried to sit up.

Ruth kept her eyes on him. She couldn't imagine why a Roman would beg for help, or why he would leave the army.

"Tell me why you are here."

The Roman nodded. "My name is Marcus. As you see, I'm a soldier. Last night I was with two other soldiers returning to our post in Jerusalem when we met an old man barely able to move along the road. My

companions thought it would be a good joke to make him carry their packs. They loaded them on his shoulders and ordered him to move along. He tried, but he fell on his knees and began to crawl on all fours like a beast of burden.

"I said this was enough and started to remove the packs from the man's back. The others stopped me. 'Let the Jew crawl,' they said. 'He should be in the dust.'

"I became angry, took off the packs, and threw them on the road. The old man disappeared in the brush by the wayside, and the soldiers went after him. I hit one hard enough to knock him out, but the other fought back.

"Defending a Jew when the law is on our side is serious. I knew I would be severely punished. So I ran away. All night I walked and crawled through the hills, not knowing where I could go or what I could do. Capture means death. And I can't go on. I am very tired."

Ruth listened intently and found herself believing the soldier's story. "Martha," she called. "Start putting the flour in the storage jar, and if anyone comes toward the house, tell me who it is immediately."

Martha could stand the strain no longer. She ran to the door and was amazed to see her mother dipping water from the water jug while the Roman sat with his head against the wall and his eyes closed.

"He's hurt," she said aloud. "And Mother is going to help him. Oh, what will happen!"

Then, knowing that her mother was counting on her, she returned to the millstone, carefully gathered up the flour, and stored it in the pottery jar which was already nearly full from the morning's work.

In a few minutes her mother came outside. "I bandaged his arm as well as I could and gave him some food and goat's milk. He was hungry and very tired. He fell asleep almost before he had eaten."

"But Mother, he can't stay here. We can't keep him in our home. What will Father say?"

51

"I don't know," her mother replied. She told Martha the young man's story. "I believe him. And he's too sick and weary to move. We'll wait and hope that no one comes searching for him before night falls. By then he may be able to go on."

Martha and Ruth spent an anxious day. They moved quietly around the house, completing their preparations for Hanukkah. But the joy and excitement were gone. At every footfall in the street they held their breath.

At last the afternoon shadows moved across the courtyard, and the welcome voice of Martha's father, Ruben, greeted them.

"Back again," he announced. "I've brought some meat for our celebration. Zebedee killed a goat and shared it with us."

Then he noticed their worried faces. "What's wrong?" he asked. "You look as though Rome had doubled our taxes!"

"It may be worse," Ruth said. Then she told her husband about the Roman soldier.

"Ruth, you're out of your mind! You know what will happen if that Roman is found in our house. You're risking all our lives to save him."

"Please, Ruben," Ruth begged. "At least listen to him. He's young, and he was injured helping one of us. I couldn't do less than he was willing to do."

"Where is he?" Ruben demanded.

"I'm here. And I will leave." The Roman appeared in the doorway, pale but more rested after his sleep.

"Stay out of sight!" Ruben ordered. "I want to talk to you."

"Martha, you keep watch," Ruth directed. "I'm going in with your father."

Martha wasn't sure whether she was glad or sorry to be left outside. Her father was upset, and she hated to see him this way. "What are we going to do?" she puzzled. "We can't have a soldier around at Hanukkah. The Romans are as bad as the Syrians were—or almost."

Martha's thoughts wandered toward the joyous celebration about to begin. A hundred years ago her people, under the brave Judas Maccabeus, had won their freedom from the Syrians. Immediately they had restored the temple in Jerusalem as a place for the worship of God.

Martha remembered the story of how Judas Maccabeus had entered the temple and found only one small jar of holy oil with which to keep the temple lamps burning. In some miraculous way, the tiny jar of oil had burned for eight days and nights until new oil could be made. Ever since then her people had celebrated this time of victory and freedom with eight days of songs and thanksgiving, feasting, and fun. And every night in Jewish homes the Hanukkah lamps were lighted, one more each evening, until eight burned brightly.

Freedom—Martha thought about the word. The Jews had not kept their freedom very long, for now Rome ruled her country.

The sound of her father's voice interrupted her thoughts. "Martha, come here."

Hurriedly, she jumped up and ran toward the door.

"Martha, your mother and I have decided to let the soldier stay with us tonight. He's too weak to walk far, and as Jews we owe him a debt for the help he has given to one of us. But this decision will require courage and secrecy. If we're caught, we shall all be punished."

Suddenly Martha knew she was glad her father had made this decision.

"Maybe they're hunting for him in Jerusalem. Maybe they won't look for him here," Martha suggested.

"I hope this is true," Ruben answered. "Now our best protection is to have our meal and then go to bed. Tomorrow Hanukkah begins, and we'll need our strength for whatever the day brings."

The Roman ate in a corner by himself. He said nothing during the meal, and watched, still silent, as Martha helped her mother unroll the sleeping mats and spread them on the floor. Ruth took a mat over to him which he accepted with a grateful smile.

Martha lay awake for a long time. Once she thought she heard soldiers marching and sat upright, straining to listen. But no one pounded on the door.

The next time she opened her eyes, daylight was streaming into the room. "Today Hanukkah begins," she remembered. The words of one of the Hanukkah psalms came to her lips,

> "O give thanks to the Lord,
> for he is good;
> his steadfast love endures for ever!"

"Martha," her mother whispered. "Marcus is still sleeping."

The events of the day before rushed back into Martha's mind. She looked toward the corner where the soldier lay. His face was flushed, and he seemed to breathe with difficulty.

"Is he sick?" she asked anxiously.

"I'm afraid he has a fever," Ruth replied.

"Is he too sick to leave?"

"I don't know yet. We're waiting until he awakens."

Silently Martha and her mother moved about the room, rolling up the sleeping mats and setting out the food for their morning meal.

Ruben had gone to the market place on the pretext of buying another lamp but actually to see if anyone were talking about a Roman deserter.

"Are they looking for him here?" Ruth questioned anxiously when Ruben returned.

"I heard nothing. What a commotion it would cause if we were to announce we had a Roman soldier as our guest!"

"Don't joke about it, Ruben," Ruth pleaded.

"My dear," he told her, "I know how serious this business is. But so far we are safe, and unless a curious neighbor stumbles onto our secret, all should go well.

"On the way back from the market I had an idea," he went on. "If he's too weak to travel, we'll ask him to wear some clothing of mine as long as he stays here, and we'll introduce him as a friend from Syria."

"From Syria?" Martha asked in surprise.

"Yes, that's his home, and that's why he speaks our language so well. He knew some Jerusalem Jews in Syria, and it was because of their friendship that he befriended another Jew."

"But he doesn't look like us," Ruth objected. "He has no beard and his eyes are blue."

"I know. The disguise won't be perfect. But he can pull a head scarf over his face and lie in a dark corner. He will be a sick guest, as indeed he is."

Martha couldn't understand her father's change in attitude. Was he glad to be protecting a Roman against the Romans?

Her father seemed to sense her bewilderment. "Yes, Martha, it's good to save a kindly person from those who would be cruel to him. And I am relieved, now that you and your mother are in no immediate danger. We'll go on with our festivities just as we always do. Tonight my brother has invited us to his home, so we will have no friends visiting us here."

The Roman stirred, and then tried to sit up. Ruth went over to him with some cool water. "How do you feel?" she asked.

"Not well," the soldier replied. "But I can't stay here and place you in more peril."

"You are not being sought in Bethlehem," Ruben assured him. "At least not yet. We're going to ask you to wear some clothing of mine through this day, and then we will see what is best to do."

Ruben supported him while Marcus slipped on the loose shirt of the Jews and wrapped the cloak around him. With a head scarf pulled across his face, he might have been anyone.

"My wife and daughter are going on about their day's work, but they will be here to bring you what you need. I must be in the fields or people will ask questions," Ruben explained. "Rest as much as you can."

Ruben left, and Ruth and Martha began their household chores. The house was swept and the Hanukkah lamps were arranged in a row before one of the windows. While Ruth mixed flour and leaven to make the flat loaves of bread the family would need, Martha went to the well for water.

She listened to the conversation of the women and the other girls as she waited her turn, but there was no talk of a missing soldier. Everyone was full of plans for Hanukkah. The women spoke of the guests they had invited and the delicacies they would serve.

The day passed quietly and uneventfully. When Ruben came home in the evening, he found a happier atmosphere awaiting him than he thought possible. Marcus was better but still weak, and his arm was badly swollen. But he seemed to be cheerful and almost enjoying his disguise. "I wish I could see myself," he remarked. "I must be a strange sight!"

After Ruben had washed his hands and face, the family gathered before the Hanukkah lamps. It was a strange beginning to the century-old celebration. While a Roman watched curiously from a corner of the room, Ruben, Ruth and Martha chanted a Hanukkah psalm, a song of victory.

> "Out of my distress I called on the LORD;
> the LORD answered me and set me free.
> With the LORD on my side I do not fear.
> What can man do to me?"

"We remember the brave words of our leader, Judas Maccabeus," Ruben said. "On the day before he went to battle he addressed his army, 'Gird yourselves and be valiant. It is better for us to die in battle than to see the misfortunes of our nation and of the sanctuary.'

"To his memory and to the hope of a free Israel we light our Hanukkah lamp."

A bright beam of light sprang from the small clay lamp, throwing the sides of the room into shadow.

"How pretty it will look from the street," Martha exclaimed. "Soon all the homes of Bethlehem will have lamps burning in their windows."

"Your freedom means much to you," said a quiet voice from the corner of the room.

Martha jumped. She had forgotten that the Roman was listening to the words of her father.

Ruben turned and spoke slowly, "Our freedom *is* of great importance to us. Our God has promised it to us in his own time. All nations who conquer us will one day have no more power, and we will be free to rule our land and to worship without the eyes of unbelievers upon us."

"By birth and by citizenship I was a Roman," Marcus replied. "But I am no longer. Now I have no country. And I, too, hope for the time when all people will have peace."

Ruben nodded. "You speak wisely and as few Romans would. But now we must leave. Ruth will give you food, and we will return when our dinner is over." Then he paused, as if uncertain about continuing. "And God keep you safely," he added.

Upsetting News

Excitement and laughter reigned in the home of Martha's uncle, Asa, when Martha and her parents entered. Martha sniffed the air. She was hungry, and the fragrance of mutton and rice, onions, and herbs made her mouth water. Asa's daughters greeted her enthusiastically.

"Let's play hopscotch. We've just time before dinner," they suggested.

The time passed quickly as the girls tossed the small stone and hopped to pick it up. Soon twilight gave way to dusk, and it was no longer possible to see the lines marked in the soft dirt. The children went into the house laughing and talking.

But inside there was no gay laughter and light conversation. Martha looked at her mother in alarm. Ruth's face was serious, and her father was clearly worried. Martha started to inquire what had happened and then caught herself in time, for her mother had shaken her head ever so slightly. The other children, however, also noticed the silence and were curious.

"Is the food burned?" they anxiously asked an older sister who was standing by the small brazier on which a pot was bubbling.

"The food is all right," she answered.

"It doesn't concern you," their mother said. "Come, we must eat."

Martha was silent during the dinner. It was not proper for children to talk when adults were conversing, so her silence was not noticed. Ruth and Ruben spoke of spring crops and household matters, but Martha knew something had happened. Were they discovered? Had her father told the story of the concealed Roman and Asa, who was a strict Jew, scolded him for giving shelter to a Gentile? Martha could only wonder.

Finally the farewells were said.

"Don't ask any questions until we are home," Ruth warned her daughter as soon as they were in the street.

The family walked along in silence, each deep in his own thoughts.

They entered the house quietly. Marcus was asleep. Ruben closed the door and threw the heavy wooden bar across it.

"Come over here," he said, moving to a corner farthest away from the sleeping man.

"We heard some bad news tonight," Ruth said. "Ruben, you tell her what Asa said."

"Asa was in Jerusalem yesterday on business, and he met a friend who has some dealings with the Romans. Asa learned that the two soldiers who were with Marcus reported the fight. The Romans believe that Marcus may have been hidden by a Jew, and they are searching every home in Jerusalem. I don't think Asa guesses Marcus is here, but he does believe the search may be continued in Bethlehem if the Roman is not found."

"How soon?" Martha asked.

"We don't know—that's the trouble."

"What will you do?"

"I'm not sure," her father answered slowly. "It will take time to search Jerusalem and the towns around there. The Romans may even look to the north before coming our way."

"Marcus can't leave tonight. He wouldn't make it as far as the hills," Ruth said.

"No, well—" Ruben hesitated. "Let's wait until morning and then we'll decide. Perhaps God will help us to know what is wise and best. We shall ask his guidance."

They bowed their heads while Ruben prayed. "O Lord, who will protect the weak and give strength to those who seek it from thee, help us in our great uncertainty. May we know what is right in your eyes and do it. Amen."

As Martha stretched out she thought, "God is greater than all the armies of the world. Surely he will help us." Then she fell asleep.

Uneasy Days

The next morning Marcus was worse. He refused food but begged constantly for water. The wound in his arm was still swollen and red. Ruth bathed his head and gave him a drink when he asked for it. She sent Martha off to the well to fill the stone water jar and to pick up any information she could. But apparently Asa had not reported his news to anyone else. Martha was sure that if the women knew the story of the missing soldier, they would be talking about it.

Back home again, Martha found her father and mother deep in a troubled conversation.

"Is Marcus' sickness God's sign that we are to keep him here?" Ruth asked her husband.

"I do not know," Ruben answered thoughtfully. "God speaks in many ways, and he may be telling us that we are to continue to care for Marcus. I wish I could be sure."

Martha guessed that her father's concern was not only for his own

61

safety. The whole family would suffer if Marcus were found in their home.

"Father," Martha said. "Doesn't the law tell us to be kind to the stranger and traveler? I'm not afraid now—not very much anyway. Let Marcus stay."

"Bless you, my daughter," Ruben answered. "I think you're right. Marcus couldn't walk ten feet from our door without fainting. But we must all be sure that we want to take the risk of keeping him here. Ruth, are you willing to continue in this danger?"

Ruth looked at her husband. She knew they were all in peril, but the punishment would fall on Ruben if Marcus were found. "I don't know. I just don't know what to do. I am not concerned for myself, but you—"

"Ruth, if this were our son, we would be sure God willed for someone to care for him," Ruben said.

Ruth was silent for several moments. At last she spoke. "Ruben, I know what you say is true. I feel it's right for us to give Marcus the care he needs. Let him stay, but oh, let nothing happen to you!"

Ruben touched his wife's arm. "I shall be cautious, but the largest responsibility will be yours and Martha's. For if I am absent from the fields the men will wonder what has happened to me. During the day you must act as though nothing unusual has happened."

Ruben threw his cloak around his shoulders. "Take care of yourselves," he said as he left.

Martha and Ruth watched him walk out into the bright winter sunshine. "At least there is no rain," Ruth commented. "We can spend the day in the courtyard and visit with our friends there if they come to call."

It was a long, anxious day, but it brought no excitement. That evening the family lit their second Hanukkah lamp with a prayer of gratitude for God's care in the past and for his help and strength in the present. Marcus watched as he had the evening before, but he made no comment.

So the days and nights passed. Five lamps were glowing in the window before Marcus' fever left, and on the sixth morning he was well enough to stand. There was still no talk in Bethlehem of a Roman who had deserted the army. The family was beginning to relax. That evening, after the sixth lamp had been lighted, Ruben, Ruth, Martha, and Marcus gathered to plan how Marcus might complete his escape.

"Do you know where you can go?" Ruben asked. "Is there any place in the world where you will be safe and able to start a new life?"

"Yes, I think so," Marcus replied. "The Roman Empire covers most of the world, but not all. To the northeast there is Parthia, which Rome has never conquered. I'm afraid, however, that I would be recognized there and treated as a spy because Parthia is an enemy of Rome. So I shall go east and south. Perhaps I can join a caravan. I've saved some money, enough to buy my food for a time. After that—who knows?"

"You don't seem worried," Ruth told him.

"How can I worry?" Marcus asked her. "A few short days ago I was all but dead. Now you have given me life and strength. I can never repay you. But I have one more favor to ask. Will you sell me the clothes I'm wearing? With them as a disguise, and with my knowledge of your language, I will have a chance to get away."

"Yes," Ruben said. "You may have the clothing, but we had better bury your own tunic and cloak. If you're caught with them, that will be the end of any escape."

"That is wise, and I'm very grateful. Tonight I will leave."

"No," Ruth said. "You're not as well as you think. If you were pursued, you wouldn't have strength to run. Stay here one more day."

"You've been in danger long enough," Marcus told her. "I know something happened while I lay ill with the fever. I cannot let you take any more chances."

"We had better tell you all we know," Ruben said. "The day after you arrived my brother Asa reported that a Roman deserter was being sought in Jerusalem and the towns nearby. The Romans think you may be hiding in some Jewish home. But there has been no alarm here, so the hunt may have turned to the north. We are not threatened, and my wife is right. You need another day of rest."

The following morning Ruben left as usual, and Ruth and Martha went about their work. When the house had been swept, the lamps filled with oil, and the day's flour ground and stored in the large clay jug, Martha and her mother picked up the water jars and went to the well together.

"We haven't seen you for a while, Ruth," the other women greeted her. "Have you been baking many Hanukkah delicacies?"

Ruth laughed. "It has been a long time, hasn't it? Now that I have a strong daughter to bring water for me I don't need to come to the well every day."

"You miss our talk," one of the women said.

Ruth nodded. "What has been happening? Are your children well?"

"Samuel is doing well in the synagogue school," one said.

Another spoke up, "Miriam broke one of my best jugs while trying to carry it on her head. But what can a mother do?"

So the conversation went. Suddenly Ruth knew that she and Martha should be home. They had left their house and Marcus too long.

Trying to act as though there were no reason to hurry, the two finally got away. Martha smiled as she lifted the heavy jug to her head. She had never broken one as Miriam had.

As they entered the dim, cool room where they lived, they heard Marcus whisper, "Is that you? Are you alone?" Ruth saw him in the darkest corner.

"What has happened?" she asked anxiously.

"I don't know," Marcus replied. "But soon after you left, someone came to the door. I moved to this corner and pretended to be asleep. Whoever it was didn't stay. I'm afraid that I was seen, though."

"Was it a man?"

"I didn't dare look."

"Shall I get Father?" Martha asked.

Worry returned to Ruth's face. "No, I don't believe that would be wise. If Ruben is called home, that would bring more questions."

"I will leave now," Marcus decided.

"No," Ruth said again. "How would I explain your presence and then your absence? We'll follow our first plan. You are a friend from Syria, and we found you here when we returned from the well. You are tired and you need rest."

"That's all true!" Martha exclaimed.

"But we won't leave you alone again," Ruth continued. "Now all we can do is wait and hope."

The day dragged along. Throughout the afternoon Ruth and Martha sat mending in the courtyard, listening for any unusual sounds in the street. But the first footsteps to turn in at the gate were Ruben's.

Inside the house, Ruth and Marcus told him what had happened.

"I can't imagine who it might have been unless a neighbor has become curious because we are celebrating Hanukkah alone," Ruben said. "Ruth, tomorrow night we must invite Asa's family here, and let this be known. But if someone has guessed what's going on, we are in trouble. There may be a reward for Marcus' capture, and too many people would welcome a chance to make some money easily."

Marcus stood up. "I'm well now," he said with decision. "My arm is almost as good at it ever was. As soon as night comes I shall start for Hebron, and there I'll join a caravan traveling toward the south. May your last day of celebration be full of joy and without fear."

"May God protect you," Ruben said.

Ruth gathered all the flat loaves of bread her family could spare and put these aside, along with handfuls of dried fruit and olives, for Marcus to take with him. Ruben brought a pair of sandals and told Marcus they were a gift.

"May they carry you to safety," he added as Marcus accepted them gratefully.

When all the preparations were finished, the seventh lamp was lighted. As Martha and her father and mother sat down for the evening meal, they noticed that Marcus had returned to the corner.

Ruth and Ruben looked at each other uncertainly. Then Ruben spoke. "I know it is the law for Jews and Gentiles not to eat together. But we have come to think of you as our friend. Will you eat with us?"

Marcus looked at them in surprise. He knew how deep was the Jewish feeling against eating with a non-Jew. He knew that their law required that the dishes used by a Gentile be destroyed. But he heard the warmth in Ruben's voice.

"I am honored to be your guest," he replied.

After the meal Martha went out into the courtyard to look at the row of Hanukkah lights. She thought about the seven days when her forefathers had waited for the new oil to be ready for the temple lamp. Were those days as filled with anxiety as these seven days had been for her family? But the oil had lasted, and she was sure Marcus would get away safely. "O God," she prayed, "go with him and protect him. Help him to know what to do."

Martha wanted to remain awake until Marcus left, but sleep overcame her.

Sometime before midnight, while she slept, a shadow moved across the room and stopped by her for a moment. There were whispered farewells, and the sound of quiet footsteps in the courtyard; then silence. And the silence lasted. No angry voices demanded the return of a runaway soldier. No harsh words ordered Ruben to follow Roman officers to prison. Finally Ruben and Ruth, too, slept quietly.

The Last Day of Hanukkah

A cock crowing in a neighbor's yard awakened Martha the next morning. She sat up, rubbing sleep from her eyes. Then she remembered and glanced across the room to the spot where Marcus had spent his time. It was empty. Her mother had already rolled up his mat.

Then she noticed something glittering on her own mat. Martha rubbed her eyes again. It was a gold coin! Martha looked up and saw her father smiling at her.

"Marcus left it for your dowry," Ruben told her. "It was his wish. He said he wanted you to have something that would help you remember an uninvited guest whom you befriended."

Martha turned the gold coin over and over in her hand. "My first dowry coin, my very first. I'll keep it always."

It was a happy, busy day with only two clouds on the horizon. Who was the person who had seen Marcus while Ruth and Martha were at the well? Where was Marcus?

The house was cleaned, the lamps again filled with oil, and more bread was baked. Ruth cooked bits of mutton with wheat groats to make a thick savory stew. Martha piled dates and figs into baskets, awaiting the evening guests.

As the sun disappeared behind the hills to the west of Bethlehem, Ruben came home. Then, to the family's surprise and alarm, there were other footsteps in the courtyard. Ruben went to the door.

"It's Asa," he called back, relief in his voice.

"I came early," Asa explained, "to meet your guest."

"Guest!" Ruben exclaimed. "There's no one here but ourselves."

"No?" Asa smiled. "I thought someone was staying with you."

"Come in," Ruben invited.

Asa entered the room and looked around. "I see he has gone."

"Who?" Ruben asked.

Then Asa laughed. "You're good at keeping secrets, my brother, but your secret is known."

Ruben didn't laugh. "Tell me what you mean."

"Known" Asa continued, "but only to me, and I will tell no one."

Ruben still remained silent. Behind him, Martha and Ruth stood, watching anxiously.

"I shouldn't alarm you, and I'm sorry if I have done so," Asa said seriously. "But when you were at our home that first evening and I reported the news of a Roman deserter, you were too quiet. I was sure you knew more than you said. Then, when my wife did not see Ruth at the well, and you did not invite us to celebrate with you as you've always done in other years, I became suspicious. Yesterday morning I came over and saw a figure in a corner of this room."

"It was you!" Ruth spoke before she thought.

Asa nodded. "The man didn't move or ask me what I wanted, so I was sure that for some reason the Roman was hiding here."

Ruben looked at his brother. "There was a man here, a friend from Syria, but he has gone. It is better if you know nothing more."

Asa shook his head to indicate he understood. "I will ask no questions. We would not welcome a Gentile into our home, nor would we befriend one of those who rule and tax us. But you must have had good reasons. Soon the others will join us. They think I came early to make arrangements for the spring plowing."

"That is well," Ruben replied. "And thank you."

The evening was a gay one. There were songs and games and laughter as the joyous Hanukkah time came to its close. Later the group walked the streets of Bethlehem singing and enjoying the Hanukkah lights.

When Asa and his family left, Ruben and Ruth and Martha sat for a few minutes around the brazier that provided welcome warmth.

"I'll never forget this Hanukkah," Martha said.

"None of us will," Ruth replied.

Ruben bowed his head, "The Lord bless us and keep us," he said. "The Lord lift up his countenance upon us and give us peace."

"And give us peace," Martha repeated. "Peace so Marcus will be safe, and we'll all be free forever."

Hanukkah was over. The oil in the lamps was almost gone, but Martha felt good inside. The Romans governed her land, and the freedom for which Judas Maccabeus had fought had not lasted. "But," Martha asked herself, "is freedom only independence from foreign armies and taxes? Can't it also be the right to be kind even to a Roman?"

Martha wasn't sure her friends would agree with her, but she liked this idea. It and Marcus would be secrets she would never tell.

MORE ABOUT HANUKKAH AND BETHLEHEM

HANUKKAH

As Martha explains in the story, Hanukkah started in Jerusalem when the Jews defeated the Syrians who had been ruling Palestine. The Syrian king had polluted the temple by sacrificing a pig—an unclean animal—on the altar. He had forbidden all Jewish worship and had further desecrated the temple by setting up an altar to pagan gods.

When Judas Maccabeus conquered the Syrians, he made a new altar of unhewn stone in accordance with the Jewish law. The seeming miracle of a small jar of oil burning for eight days gave rise to Hanukkah, which is sometimes called the "Feast of Dedication," in celebration of the cleansed temple; or the "Feast of Lights," in memory of the burning flame of the temple lamp.

Hanukkah is still celebrated in Jewish homes today. It is a happy festival with games, songs, special foods, and gifts. On the first evening a single candle is lit, and on each succeeding night others are added until eight are burning. The hymn "Rock of Ages" is often sung after the candles have been lit.

Psalm 118 is a song of thanksgiving often used on festival occasions. The verses Martha and her family repeat in the story are from this psalm. The words of Judas Maccabeus are from *1 Maccabees 3:58a, 59* in the Apocrypha.

In *John 10:22* you will find a reference to Hanukkah in Jesus' day.

Rock of Ages

Leopold Stein

Translated by M. Jastrow and G. Gottheil

1. Rock of A - ges, let our song Praise thy sav - ing pow - er;
2. Kin - dling new the ho - ly lamps, Priests ap-proved in suf - fer - ing,
3. Chil - dren of the mar - tyr race, Wheth - er free or fet - tered,

Thou, a - midst the rag - ing foes, Wast our shel-t'ring tow - er.
Pu - ri - fied the na - tion's shrine, Brought to God their of - fer - ing.
Wake the ech - oes of the songs Where ye may be scat - tered!

Fu - rious they as - sailed us, But thine arm a - vailed us,
And his courts sur - round - ing Hear, in joy a - bound - ing,
Yours the mes - sage cheer - ing, That the time is near - ing

And thy word Broke their sword, When our own strength failed us.
Hap - py throngs Sing-ing songs Far and wide re - sound - ing.
Which shall see All men free, Ty-rants dis - ap - pear - ing A - men.

BETHLEHEM

Bethlehem, where the Martha of this might-have-happened story lived, was an old city when the first Hanukkah festival was celebrated in 165 B.C.

Perhaps someday you will visit Bethlehem. If you do, you will find it about seven miles south of Jerusalem. It is a small city, but its name is as well known as any city in the world. Here are some biblical events that took place in Bethlehem.

Many hundred years before Jesus was born, the Jewish people were independent with a king of their own. The first king's name was Saul, but he was not always a wise or a good ruler. So Samuel, a religious leader, went to Bethlehem to find a king who would follow Saul. In Bethlehem Samuel talked to a man named Jesse who had eight sons. One of these sons was to be chosen king. You can read this story and learn the name of a great king of the Jewish people in *1 Samuel 16:1–13*.

There are two stories about the birth of Jesus. Both stories tell us that he was born in Bethlehem. The first story is in *Matthew 2:1–12*. The second is in *Luke 2:1–20*.

71

Going to Jerusalem

Juda moved restlessly as he sat on the cold floor of the Capernaum synagogue. Around him rose the rhythmic chanting of his schoolmates, reciting passages from the law which the rabbi had assigned. Automatically Juda's lips formed the words, but his mind was far away, as far away as Jerusalem. Would his father know about the trip when he returned home this evening? How soon would he be sure?

"Juda!"

Juda jumped at the sound of his name.

"Sit quietly," the rabbi ordered. "You are as restless as a flea this morning."

"He'd be restless, too, if he knew," Juda muttered to himself.

Juda glanced at the other boys who were trying to hide their grins and then forced his mind to return to the lesson.

The long morning finally passed, and the boys ran out into the warm air. Juda was stopped by his friend, Benjamin.

"What was the matter with you this morning?" Benjamin asked.

"Oh, nothing," Juda replied. He couldn't tell anyone, not even Benjamin, until he was sure. "I knew that passage. It was hard to pay attention."

"You know something else, and you won't tell," Benjamin accused him. "What is it?"

"Nothing. Come on. Let's get away from here."

The two boys walked up the street toward their homes and the midday meals that awaited them.

All afternoon Juda roamed restlessly around the courtyard of his home, paying little attention to his mother and sisters, Leah and Mary, who were baking bread. When his younger brother, David, begged him to play with him, Juda ignored him. He even refused Benjamin's invitation to go for a walk along the lake shore.

Just when Juda was sure he could stand it no longer, he heard his father's footsteps in the street.

"Father," he called, rushing to the door. "Father, have you heard? Are we going?"

Nathan paused on the threshold to touch the mezuzah reverently as he entered, then smiled as he saw the eager look on his son's face. "Yes, Juda, I have good news for you. I will need to make the trip to Jerusalem. And now that you are eleven and David is nine, you are old enough to go with me. But we'll have to ask the rabbi if you two can miss a week or so of school."

Juda was alarmed. "Father, the rabbi is angry with me because I couldn't be still. But I know the lessons. You'll make him let me go?"

"I think it can be arranged," his father smiled.

"When will we start?"

"In a day or so. Now go and play while I talk with your mother."

Juda could hardly contain himself. Nothing so exciting had ever happened. In fact, he had never been away from Capernaum. He thought

of the temple in Jerusalem, of the palace of Herod with its rooms for
a hundred guests, of the shops and the people that he would soon be
seeing. He rushed out into the street and ran to Benjamin's house to
tell him the good news. But Benjamin was not there.

"Where is he?" Juda asked Benjamin's mother.

"I'm not sure," she replied. "He was going to the lake to see the
fishing boats."

"Thanks. I'll find him," Juda called as he turned in the direction
of the Sea of Galilee.

As Juda ran toward the lake, the familiar smell of fish and fishing
boats became stronger. The boats were in now, and the early morning
catch had long since been unloaded. Most of the fish were sold to the
fish-pickling factory at the southern end of the lake. His father's business
was to see that the pickled fish were shipped all over the Roman Empire.

"Benjamin," Juda called again and again as he walked along the
shore. But Benjamin did not appear. Finally, when it was close to the
dinner hour, Juda returned home. He must have missed Benjamin.
Tomorrow would have to be soon enough to share his exciting news.

That night Juda went to sleep with thoughts of the coming trip
uppermost in his mind. Sometime later he was awakened by the sound
of his father's voice.

"Juda, come here quickly."

Surprised and a little alarmed, Juda sat up on his sleeping cot. It
was dark and cool. Hastily slipping on his sandals, he ran out into the
courtyard.

"What's the matter?" he asked anxiously when he saw Benjamin's
parents standing there with his own father and mother.

"Did you see Benjamin this afternoon?" they asked.

"No," Juda replied. "I couldn't find him. Where is he?"

"We don't know," Benjamin's mother said. She looked tired and
worried. "We have waited all evening for him to come home, but he

74

hasn't appeared. I thought you might know where he is."

"I don't. Do you suppose he went out on the lake, and the boat hasn't come back?"

"He'd never do that without telling me. And we've talked to the fishermen. One man saw him walking toward the hills, but that's the last news we've had."

Juda was worried. Benjamin was his best friend. What could have happened to him?

"We've got to get home," Benjamin's mother said. "Let us know if you hear anything, anything at all."

Benjamin's mother and father left, and Juda turned to his own parents. "Let me search the hills. He might be in a cave with a sprained ankle or a broken arm or something."

Nathan looked at his son's troubled face. "It won't do any good to hunt in the dark. We'll have to wait until daylight. You go back to sleep, and we'll hope Benjamin turns up in the next hour or so."

For what seemed like a long time Juda lay awake listening for the sound of voices that would indicate some news, but the house and the courtyard were silent. "O King of the universe," he prayed, "where is Benjamin? Take care of him. Help us to find him."

Sometime later Juda was awakened by his father's voice. "It's daylight, and we can help now. Some neighbors are joining us. We may have a long search ahead, and we need you to show us where you and Benjamin like to go."

Juda was glad to be needed, and he hurried out with his father. His mother had some dates, figs, and bread ready for them to eat.

For several hours the group searched, first along the lake where the boats were coming in after a night of fishing, then in the hills, among the orchards and through the streets of the city. Even at this early hour many people were up, but no one had seen a boy of eleven wearing a brown cloak and leather sandals.

Finally, Nathan sent Juda back to the synagogue school. "You can't do any more here," he said. "And besides, some of the boys may have information about Benjamin."

But none of the boys had any clues, and that morning the rabbi had a difficult time keeping his pupils' minds on their lessons.

"It won't help Benjamin for you not to learn," he told them. "The men are doing all that can be done. And Benjamin is in God's care. We must remember that."

A weary Nathan appeared for the evening meal that night. He found his wife and children anxiously waiting. "There is no trace of him," he reported. "We've looked everywhere. Benjamin has vanished. All we can do now is to wait and hope. Tomorrow I must leave for Jerusalem. Do you still want to go, Juda and David? Or do you want to remain here? I've talked to the rabbi, and he has given you permission to miss school."

Juda had been wondering about the trip. He wanted to go badly, but he felt guilty about leaving.

David waited for his older brother to speak, but it was clear from the expression on his face that he wanted to make the trip.

"Father, what should I do?" Juda asked. Then he had an idea. "Do you think we might hear any news on the trip?"

"I don't know," Nathan answered. "We might. And I don't think we can do any more in Capernaum."

"I do want to go, but I hate to be away when Benjamin is found. It's like deserting him."

"I think he would understand, and Benjamin's parents are glad I'm going. They believe I might possibly hear some word about him."

"Let's go," David pleaded. "Leah and Mary can look some more around here."

Juda nodded, wishing he could be as excited about the trip as he had been twenty-four hours earlier. "We'll ask everyone we see. Someone must know where he went."

Unexpected Excitement

Preparations were quickly made. Juda knew they would join others on the journey, for few people chose to travel alone. Thieves were too numerous, and the best protection against them was to travel in a good-sized group.

Before they left early the next morning, Juda went over to his friend's home. Benjamin's father was awake, looking tired and worried. Juda knew he had learned nothing more.

"I'll find out anything I can," Juda promised.

"I know you will," Benjamin's father told him. "The Lord go with you and protect you."

"The Lord is very great and very powerful," Juda responded. Then he added, "The Lord be with you."

The first day of travel was easy and fun. The road skirted the edge of Galilee before making its long descent down the Jordan Valley to the south. Juda's and David's eyes took in all the new sights.

On the second day the party passed through the large Greek city of Scythopolis. Juda was puzzled by a tall mound rising near the town. "What's that?" he asked his father.

"It's all that is left of the ancient city," Nathan replied. "Near there the Israelites were defeated by the Philistines and the dead bodies of King Saul and his son Jonathan were hung on the city walls."

"Father, why did God let this happen to a king of our people?"

"Saul was not a good man in his later life," Nathan answered. "He did wrong, so he died."

"But does God always punish people who do wrong? Did Benjamin do wrong? Is that why we can't find him?"

"I don't know, my son," Nathan said. "I don't believe God is punishing Benjamin."

Juda was thoughtful as he walked along. This was a new idea. He couldn't believe that Benjamin had done anything that would cause God to punish him and bring so much worry to his family and friends. But Juda couldn't put the thought out of his mind. Where was Benjamin? What had happened to him?

It grew steadily warmer as the road dipped lower and lower into the valley. Sleeping under the stars that night was very comfortable. As Juda dropped off, his rolled-up cloak serving as a pillow, his last thoughts were anxious ones. Was God caring for Benjamin or punishing him? Would he ever find out what had happened to his friend?

The stars were still visible and the sun had not yet appeared when the travelers started on the third day of their trip. Already it was warm, and it grew hot before many miles had been covered. Walking was difficult. Juda's feet ached, and he wondered if David felt as sticky as he did.

The group moved on. They passed no more large towns, but everywhere the boys could see fields of grain and orchards of fig and date trees.

Nathan and Juda questioned everyone they saw about Benjamin, but no one had any information.

On the fourth morning Nathan announced that this was the last day they would be traveling in the Jordan Valley. Tomorrow they would spend the sabbath in Jericho and then begin the climb to Jerusalem. The group quickened its pace as it moved along the caravan route, with the heavy vegetation marking the path of the Jordan River on one side and the barren wilderness of Judah on the other.

Juda and David paused for a moment to watch a lizard scuttle away beneath a rock. "He is wise and lucky," Juda told his brother. "He knows where to find shade."

"And he can get in it," David answered. "I don't see any rocks that are our size."

Suddenly there were angry shouts ahead. The two boys looked up and gasped. "Robbers!" David exclaimed.

"You stay here," Juda told him. "I've got to help." He picked up

a rock and ran toward the men. Juda's father and the others were having a hard time. The robbers were beating the members of the party with heavy sticks and trying to snatch off the girdles in which the travelers carried their money.

Juda threw his rock at one of the robbers with all the force he had. His aim was good. The man dropped what he had taken and clutched his shoulder in pain. Then, seeing that a boy was attacking, him, he raised his stick and started toward Juda, who looked frantically around for another rock. None of those around was large enough to do any good, so Juda started to run. But he stopped in surprise when he saw that the man had been hit again. David had entered the fight and his aim, like Juda's, had been good.

"David, look out," Juda shouted as the robber started toward the younger boy. David turned, but too late. The heavy stick came down against his arm at the same moment that Juda threw himself on the man. Caught off balance, the man stumbled, and Juda grabbed his stick.

By this time, Juda's father and the others, who had the advantage of numbers, were getting control of the situation. The attackers, realizing that they were beaten, escaped into the barren hills.

"They must have been desperate to take on a group our size," one of the men remarked.

"There probably are few opportunities for their kind of work along this road when people travel in groups," Nathan said. "David, let me see your arm."

His father felt the arm gently. "I think that you're fortunate, David. You have a bad bruise, and it may be several days before you can use your arm easily, but the bone isn't broken. I'm glad that you won't have to travel tomorrow. You boys made me proud of you, but I don't want to repeat this experience."

Nathan made a sling for David's injured arm and then joined the men who were considering what to do next. Juda took the bundle of food David had been carrying and added it to his own load. When Nathan returned he gave directions.

"Juda, you and David are to walk in the middle of the group. We'll all keep our eyes and ears open. There may be more people along here eager to get money without working for it."

The party moved off, more slowly now because David found that walking hurt his arm. For the rest of the day's journey there were no alarms and no signs of further trouble. Everyone welcomed the sabbath rest in Jericho.

The last miles of the trip were made over the regular route from Jericho to Jerusalem. The green banks of the Jordan were now behind them. Juda and David were awed and almost frightened by the desolate

country through which they walked. Heat and dust and weariness added to their discomfort. But all this was forgotten when, toward sundown, they climbed the final steep slope of the Mount of Olives and saw before them their holy city, Jerusalem. The temple caught the rays of the setting sun and shone like gold against the blue sky.

Nathan broke into song and was quickly joined by the others:

"Pray for the peace of Jerusalem!
'May they prosper who love you!
Peace be within your walls,
and security within your towers!'"

Juda kept his eyes on the city ahead as he walked along. Through his mind moved the names of the great men who had been in Jerusalem— David, Nehemiah, Jeremiah. They were his people, leaders of his nation. Now he, too, was to see the holy city. He forgot that he was tired. He wanted to run toward the heavy gates in the massive stone walls, but he knew that David was too tired to hurry. "We'll soon be there, David," he said, "and you can rest as long as you wish. Your arm will feel better when you won't have to walk every day."

David nodded. "But tomorrow I want to go with you to see the city. And we can ask about Benjamin."

"Benjamin!" Juda exclaimed. "David, I forgot about him. I'll start asking tonight."

Nathan and David and Juda went to the home of a business friend of Nathan's where they were to stay during their visit in Jerusalem. Josiah, their host, welcomed them warmly and introduced them to his wife and his only son, Eber, who was a year younger than Juda but almost as tall. Eber promised to be their guide around the city while the men took care of business matters.

When Juda told Eber about Benjamin, Eber was interested. "We'll inquire together," he promised. "Someone may know something. You know, it's strange, but another man was here not long ago and said that two boys had disappeared from Nazareth. No one could find them either."

"That *is* strange," Juda replied.

"Well, we can't start asking tonight," Eber said. "But the first thing tomorrow we'll begin."

The group gathered for the evening meal, and Josiah bowed his head. "Bless thou this food, O Lord, King of the Universe," he prayed. "May we eat it in thankfulness together. In the name of our Lord, Jesus Christ. Amen."

Juda caught a startled and disturbed look on his father's face. Nathan half rose, and for a minute Juda thought his father was going to leave the room. Then Nathan settled back and ate slowly, but he was quiet. It was the boys who kept the conversation going. Once Juda noticed his father looking at Josiah thoughtfully. "Our Lord, Jesus Christ," Juda repeated to himself. "This is not in our prayer. I wonder why Josiah said that?"

But he found himself too tired to wonder very long. He was glad when Josiah suggested that they go to bed early.

Jerusalem!

The next morning the boys started their exploration. Juda and David had seen many people in Capernaum, but never anything like the crowds that jostled one another in the Jerusalem streets.

"First, we'll go out across the Kidron to the Mount of Olives where you can see the city in the morning light. That's the view I like best. Then I'll take you on the big tour," Eber suggested.

When they had passed outside the city gates and climbed part way up the Mount of Olives, Juda noticed a huge oval-shaped building.

"What's that?" he asked.

"Herod's amphitheatre," Eber replied. "Athletic games and horse races are held there. The Jewish people were angry when it was built."

"Over there is the Garden of Gethsemane," Eber went on. "Now we'll go back into the city, and I'll show you Herod's palace, the gymnasium, the fortress, and anything else you wish."

The boys spent a busy morning roaming over the city. Juda was delighted with the buildings; many were white, a contrast to the somber colors of the Capernaum homes.

Juda did not forget Benjamin. He and Eber told the story to a number of Eber's friends and asked if they had heard anything. No one had. When the sun was high in the sky, and the boys were feeling hungry, they returned to Eber's home.

In the evening Nathan said they would remain in Jerusalem one more day, and then they must start the return journey to Capernaum.

"But Father," Juda protested. "You promised to take us to the temple, and we haven't heard a thing about Benjamin. Can't we stay longer?"

"No, Juda," Nathan replied. "I must get back. We have a long trip ahead, as you well know, and a large caravan is leaving for Capernaum on the day after tomorrow. I'm arranging for us to go with them. But tomorrow morning we will go to the temple."

Good News

The next morning when Nathan and David and Juda reached the Court of the Gentiles which surrounded the temple, the place was already crowded with people hurrying to and fro. Juda looked around the vast open area. He saw that the court was enclosed on four sides by porches, the roofs of which were supported by beautiful columns. Nathan said that the porch on the east side was named Solomon's porch after the king who had built the first temple.

But Juda's eyes were caught by the temple itself. It was built of snow-white stone and occupied a position of importance in the northern part of the court. The stone was set off with panels of gold, and the roof was studded with gilded pinnacles. It was far more beautiful than anything Juda had imagined.

"We can go into the Women's Court," Nathan told them. "And when you are older you may come with me into the Court of Israel and take part in the great sacrifice."

In the Women's Court David noticed some large wooden chests.

"What are these?" he asked.

"Those are for the temple offerings," Nathan replied. He gave the boys some coins, and they each deposited their money in the chests. As Juda put in his coins he felt proud and important—his money would help to keep the temple beautiful.

"The inner court is the Court of Israel," Juda's father went on. "From there you can see the sacrifices being offered in the Priest's Court. But no one may see the Holy of Holies except the high priest, and he goes in only once a year. It is our most sacred place."

Juda was silent, awed by the magnificence and importance of the spot where he stood. He was sorry when his father said they must go.

As they stepped again into the glare of the Court of Gentiles, a young man approached them.

"Are you Nathan from the city of Capernaum?" the young man asked.

"Yes," Nathan responded. "But I don't recognize you."

"I had better remain unknown," the man replied quietly. "But I come as a friend with news about the boy your son and Eber have been seeking. He is here, near Jerusalem. Soon he and other boys like him will be taken away to be sold as slaves to wealthy men in the East."

"How do you know? Where is Benjamin?" Juda asked excitedly.

"My brother is a leader among those who hold the boys," the young man replied. "I was with him until last week when I was injured in a fight and left by the roadside. A follower of the prophet called Jesus found me and cared for me. From this man I learned a new way of thinking and acting. My brother does not know that I am alive, and soon I'll be leaving for Damascus where I'll be safe. The boy you seek is three Roman miles down the Bethlehem road in a camp that stands on the hillside off to the left of the road."

Then, before Nathan or Juda could say more, the young man disappeared in the crowd.

"What shall we do?" Juda exclaimed. "How can we rescue Benjamin?"

"We must ask Josiah," his father said. "He'll know where to get help. And we must act quickly."

The three hurried away from the temple area, back to the home of Nathan's friend. There they told their story.

"You say this young man claimed to be a follower of Jesus of Nazareth?" Josiah asked.

"Yes," Nathan replied. "That's what he told us."

"Then we can trust him. I know some men who will help us. Let me make the arrangements."

Josiah was away for over an hour. When he returned he said that all was ready. "Eber, it's best for you and Juda and David to remain here. Nathan, we're joining some others who know how to act in a situation like this. Eber, you tell your mother what has happened, and ask her not to worry. God will be with us. Now let's be on our way."

When Eber's mother returned from the market, the boys told her all that had happened. She was concerned but not as troubled as Juda knew his own mother would have been.

The hours dragged by. When the afternoon shadows fell across the city, Juda felt he could stand it no longer. "What is happening?" he asked over and over again. "Will they find Benjamin? Will he be hurt?" But no one could answer his questions except a group of men who were on the Bethlehem road.

The Story

Night came, and still there was no sign of Nathan and Josiah. Juda, Eber, David, and Eber's mother gathered in a room of Eber's home where they sat around a pottery brazier, glad for its warmth in the cool night air. The boys were restless and anxious. Suddenly David exclaimed, "They're coming, I hear them!"

They hurried to the door which was opened before they reached it. Juda and David gave a shout of welcome as they saw Benjamin. Then they stopped in surprise. With him were three other boys.

"Juda, David!" Benjamin exclaimed. "It's good to see you! I never thought we'd meet in Jerusalem!"

"And are we glad to see you!" Juda responded. "What happened? Where have you been? Are you all right?"

"Yes, we all are," Benjamin answered. "These are my friends who were with me in the camp. The bandits took good care of us because they wanted us to be in fine condition when we were sold. Slaves—that's what we were to be!"

"Father, are you hurt? What *did* happen? Was there a fight?" Juda grasped his father's arm and held on tightly.

"Easy there, Juda," Nathan replied. "We'll tell you the whole story while we're having something to eat."

Eber's mother brought rice and meat and goat's milk. Everyone sat around the mat on which she placed the food.

Nathan began the story, "A group of outlaws started what would have been a profitable business if they had been successful. They made their living by robbing travelers and stealing animals, but they added a sideline of kidnapping boys. There is a good market for boy slaves in countries a safe distance from here. Only one or two boys were taken from a city so there would be no organized search. Ezra and John are from Jericho and Peter lives in Tiberias."

"When we reached the camp of the outlaws, we hid for a while to learn how many men were in the camp and to plan our strategy for making the rescue."

"You certainly came at the right time," Benjamin declared. "There were only three guards with us this afternoon."

"We didn't have any trouble," Nathan agreed. "When our party of twelve marched into the camp, the guards left in a hurry. We found all the boys together in one tent."

"Bound and gagged," Benjamin added. "They took out the gags only when we ate, and then just one at a time, while they held a stick over us so we wouldn't dare call out. My mouth is still sore!"

"That's about it," Nathan said. "Benjamin can tell you more on our way home."

"Were there other boys?" David asked.

"Yes," Ezra told him. "There were fifteen of us. The others will go with caravans traveling toward their homes, just as we're going with you."

"But how did they get you?" Eber asked Benjamin.

"They grabbed me while I was walking in the hills behind Capernaum. I went farther than I meant to. I guess I was mad at you, Juda, for not telling me your secret."

Juda looked ashamed. "I'm sorry, Benjamin, but I really couldn't tell you about the trip until I was sure."

"We were lucky to meet that man while we were in the temple today," David said.

"Yes, you were," Josiah agreed.

Nathan turned to his friend. "You were certain we could trust him because he said he was a follower of Jesus of Nazareth. I have heard of these followers. People say that they are not keeping our sacred law, that they are dangerous."

Josiah looked thoughtful and a little sad. "I am one of these dangerous men. Eber and his mother are followers and so are those who helped us today. We do not try to disobey the law, but we do not think that just keeping the law is the way to serve God best."

Nathan was deeply disturbed. "What you say is hard for me to understand. How do you serve God if you don't rely on the law to tell you his holy will?"

"By loving and helping our fellowmen," Josiah replied.

"That's what we try to do too," Nathan told his friend.

"One of the differences," Josiah said, "is that when we must choose between the law and service, we choose service. If someone a distance away needs our help on the sabbath day, we walk that distance to give what aid we can."

Juda was listening to every word. What Josiah said seemed right to him, and yet the law was important. It was God's law given to his people. How could anyone dare to disobey it?

"Did Jesus tell you to break the law?" Juda asked.

"No," Josiah told him. "But he did teach us that God cares more about his people than about his law."

Juda and David looked anxiously at their father who seemed lost in thought. Benjamin and the three boys with him were listening to the conversation intently. After a time, Nathan spoke again.

"You've been a good and brave friend, Josiah. Today you risked your life to help me find a boy who was lost. But I cannot accept what you say about Jesus. He may have been very wise, but he is not wiser than all the leaders and prophets of our people."

Josiah nodded. "Many feel as you do, and I respect you for being loyal to the truth you accept. Perhaps we have talked enough tonight, for tomorrow you start a long trip. These boys must be very tired."

The group settled for the night. Benjamin unrolled a sleeping mat beside Juda, and was soon sound asleep. But Juda lay awake for a while, thinking about the things he had just heard. "How does God let people know what is true?" he asked himself. "How can a person be sure?"

Home Again

Five days later those in the caravan caught their first sight of the Sea of Galilee. Benjamin wanted to run toward the blue water, but he knew he still had many miles to walk. The party trudged on. At long last, the gray buildings of Capernaum came into view.

"Home!" Benjamin exclaimed. "I thought I'd never see it again!"

"We'll go to your house first," Nathan said. "I wish we could have saved your parents some anxious days by sending word that you were with us, but there was no way."

"There's my house!" Now Benjamin did run up the sloping street toward the low building where he lived.

"Father, Mother," he called. "I'm here. Nathan found me."

His parents rushed to the door. "Benjamin, my son!" his father cried as he ran to meet him.

"What happened? Where were you?" his parents asked together.

"In Jerusalem," he told them. "Nathan rescued me from bandits."

Benjamin's father looked at Nathan. "Your boy gives me too much credit," Nathan said. "Benjamin was kidnapped, but there were other men with me when we found him. He will tell you the story."

"I'll see you soon," Juda called as they left.

It was a glad homecoming for Nathan's family. Mary and Leah had to hear everything several times. Their mother looked anxiously at David when she heard about the injury to his arm.

David pretended to punch his brother. "It's well now," he assured her with a grin.

Later in the evening the family went up to the roof of their home and sat looking at the stars in the night sky.

"Father," Juda said, "I guess you didn't know what kind of a trip we would have!"

"I didn't," Nathan agreed.

"And if we hadn't gone, and if Eber hadn't asked his friends about Benjamin, we might never have rescued him."

"It turned out for the best," Nathan said.

"I'd like to see Jerusalem again," Juda continued. "I'd like to go for the Passover in the spring. And I want to see Eber. Do you think we can?"

"Perhaps. But that's some time away. Tomorrow you must go back to school. You have missed too many lessons."

"School!" Juda and David muttered. But they were not unwilling. Even the rabbi would be interested in their trip to Jerusalem. What a lot they would have to tell!

MORE ABOUT CAPERNAUM AND JERUSALEM

CAPERNAUM

The Capernaum of Juda's day was located on the northern shore of the Sea of Galilee. It may have had 50,000 people. Certainly it was a large city, for the Roman government had a customs house and a number of troops there.

The people made their living chiefly through fishing and farming. Fruit trees, olive orchards, and vineyards covered the hillsides. Fishing boats moved out into the lake every morning. Their catch was sold for food and to the fish-pickling factory farther down the lake. Pickled fish from Capernaum were sent to towns all over the Roman Empire.

The buildings were not made of mud brick and stone, as was true of other Palestinian towns, but of black lava bricks quarried from the surface of nearby hills. The synagogue, however, may have been built of lighter-colored stones and probably stood on the same site where the ruins of a synagogue may be seen today. The synagogue was higher than any private house, for there was a law that no other building could "look down on" the synagogue. It was this building that travelers would see first as they came near the city.

Capernaum was well known to Jesus. From our New Testament we learn that he lived there for a time and spoke in the synagogue. You can read about this in *Matthew 4:12–14* and *Mark 1:21–22*.

From Luke we learn that the synagogue in Capernaum was built by a Roman soldier, a centurion, who came to Jesus for help when the centurion's slave was ill. See *Luke 7:1–10* for this story.

JERUSALEM

Jerusalem was more important than any other city to the Jews of the first century. Politically it was important because it was their capital city, but it was also their holy city where the temple was located. Every Jewish boy wanted to see Jerusalem more than any other place in the world.

Two thousand years ago Jerusalem was already an old city. Hundreds of years before Jesus lived, King David made it his capital. Solomon, David's son, built the first temple there. Because Jerusalem was the Jewish capital, every enemy invading Palestine tried to capture it, and it was destroyed and rebuilt many times.

Christians are deeply interested in Jerusalem because so many events in the life of Jesus took place there.

*Camels traveling through the wilderness on the road from
Jerusalem down to Jericho.*

The Jordan River as seen from an airplane.

Jerusalem still exists today. It stands on a hill about 2,550 feet above sea level. Because of its location it is much cooler than Jericho and Capernaum. Snow may fall there in the winter months, and rain is common between October and April. The present walls surrounding part of Jerusalem are of stone and were rebuilt less than a thousand years ago. The city inside the walls is often called the "old city."

If you visited Jerusalem, you would not see the buildings Juda saw. Whatever may remain of these buildings lies buried about thirty feet beneath the level of the present city. Each time Jerusalem was destroyed, the ruins of the buildings were smoothed down, and new buildings were constructed on top of what remained of the old. So gradually, over the centuries, the ground level of the city grew higher and higher. But you would be able to see some of the stones that were used by King Herod's builders in the first century, giant blocks measuring from over three to as much as fourteen feet in length. These stones are in the ancient Wailing Wall, shown to every pilgrim and tourist.

In the Bible, you can read of important events that took place in Jerusalem. Here are a few.

Under David, Jerusalem became the capital city of the Jews. See *2 Samuel 5: 1–5*. It was the city in which the first temple was built by Solomon, who became king after David. This story is in *2 Chronicles 3:1–2*. Some of the psalms show the feeling of the people for Jerusalem. The song which Nathan sings in the story is from *Psalm 122:6–7*.

Jerusalem was the city in which Jesus spent the final week of his life. If you want to read about some of the events of this week, you will find the stories in the following Bible passages:

The story of the triumphal entry: *Matthew 21:1–11*.
The last supper with his disciples: *Matthew 26:17–30*.
The crucifixion: *Matthew 27:33–50*.
The resurrection: *Mark 16:1–8*.

How to Pronounce Names That May Be New to You

In "A Journey into Time"
    Joshua—jah' shoo ah
    Khirbet Qumran—kir' bet koom ran'
    Mahmud—mah' mood
    Moab—moe' ab
In "The Missing Coin"
    Ahab—ay' hab
    Esdraelon—es' drah ee' lon
    Jared—jair' ed
    Jerusalem—je roo' sa lem
    Obed—oh' bed
In "The Strange Guest"
    Asa— ay' sa
    Hanukkah—ha' nu kah
    Marcus—mar' kus
    Ruben—roo' ben
In "Going to Jerusalem"
    Benjamin—ben' ja min
    Eber—ee' ber
    Herod—hair' od
    Josiah—jo si' ah
    Juda—joo' dah
    Leah—lee' ah
    Nathan—nay' than
    Capernaum—ka pur' nay um
    Scythopolis—si thah' pol is